Gypsy Flamenco

Gypsy Flamenco

A Novel

Dolores de Leon

Ashland Hills Press

Book design by Nancy Parker

Front cover photo, "Shoes," by Nancy Bardos.

ISBN 0-9642272-6-6

Published by Ashland Hills Press, P.O. Box 992, Ashland, OR 97520
Phone 541-951-1129

Library of Congress Control Number: 2013930090

Author's web site: www.DoloresdeLeon.com

First Edition.

Printed in the United States of America.

To
Larry
(1929-1991)

It wasn't night
Or afternoon
The air was pale
     yellow
It must have been
     morning

The flamenco singer
Sitting in a straight
     black chair
Her face
A fan of wrinkles

Having sung all night
Narrowed her voice
And broke open the
     dawn

I could speak then
Tell you about
The tall gentle-eyed
     man
Who had held my flesh
Shed his tears with
     mine
Breathed into the palm
     of my hand

Tell you
He has taken
The long train
Across the last
     bridge

But in my memory
He is young
     again

He laughs and smiles
     again
While I turn only
     half my face
To the world.

                    —DdL, 2010

TABLE OF CONTENTS

INTRODUCTION

YA NO EXISTE

Mornings in Sevilla. Roses replaced the Goya night and the air hung by a thread on the narrow, winding streets between the slanted houses; memories of horses clopped on the cobblestones.

The streets were empty and I had a dance lesson to go to, like a kid taking ballet classes. Only in Spain I was fifty-five years old but still hopeful, still looking through the sun.

Placing each foot towards the studio, I'd take a shortcut down an alleyway to Calle Matamoros. On the corner a building faced out like the prow of a ship. My destination was the small flamenco studio of maestro Pio Mateo Mendoza, its walls covered with photographs of him. And the one window, by a green curtain with orange polka dots the size of my fist.

The *tic-tac* of heels would already be in progress. Sounds of De Falla coming from a piano across the street would mix with Pio's own small heels pounding out the *compás*, the accents of flamenco: three, six, eight, ten, twelve.

Next came greeting Pio and dealing with whatever his mood might be: "Look, look Doloré. Look at the photographs. There. There I am in Paris. There I am in Madrid. I was phenomenal! The best flamenco dancer ever!"

Or, "Look. Look, Doloré, there's old Caracol and Terremoto and Marchena. The great ones. But they're all gone. I'm the only one left, and nobody knows who I am, who I was. It's all over. I'm closing the studio, Doloré. Now. Today."

"Pio, I've paid you in advance!"

An argument would ensue. But once the argument was over, I'd hear my own heels driving the rhythms into the floor. The *compás* of flamenco would become my heartbeat.

Around the *compás* orbit the many moons of flamenco music—the muezzin's call to the faithful, the rabbis intoning the Torah, the Gregorian chants of the Mozarabics, the chattering ankle bells of northern Spain.

I could hear them all in the guitar.

When the guitar becomes sweet and old, I cry most for the *antiqua* style of flamenco. Pio recreated this gracious, old flamenco on students such as myself.

But Pio himself? He was not gracious. Blustering, boastful, lecherous, running like a tomcat through the streets of Sevilla to scratch at bar doors for a free drink, he was an arrogant, impecunious little Gypsy with an egg-shaped balding head, face pointed up, his big hook nose slapping at the sunlight. Usually he walked alone because those that knew him, wished they didn't.

Yet it was Pio's choreography that scorched me to tears, the arms rising and falling like fountain spray, torsos weaving the interlacing lines on Moorish walls, wrists circling, fingers drawing flowers in the air. His own small feet holding the rhythms that became words, setting my heels to follow his.

~

When my morning lesson was over, sweat filled the studio and the dressing room, that dank hallway to nowhere. With sweat in my hair, I would go to the Bar Robles for something swift and cold to drink.

The streets by then were no longer morning.

Cars filled and choked Sevilla, banged and bumped the

sidewalks, chipped away at the five-hundred-year-old buildings, chipped away at the living ghosts. Everyone like Pio, living through the present by means of the past. And it was gone.

Ya no existe.

· 1 ·

DUENDE

My plane left Kennedy International July third, 1985, at eight PM. Two hours later, I met dawn over an ocean, no boundaries, no land.

~

Madrid. My first night, July fourth, up four flights with my luggage. An all-white room too hot with the windows closed, too noisy with them open. A traffic jam on the Gran Via at 3 a.m.; my night burned with no sleep.

I was staying at the Hostal Salinas, a *pensión* run by Mama and Papa Salinas just to house their visiting relatives. I was the only 'guest.' All doors were open to the hallway. We helped ourselves in the kitchen.

At night, while Mama Salinas crocheted fine lace flowers in the dark, I watched televison. A concert from the Royal Palace of Sevilla, and the quiet voice of the guitar explaining Spain's mistakes told me Sevilla was where I wanted to be.

I had planned a week to pack in museums, see old friends, practice my lisping *theta*. But instead, I promised Mama Salinas I would be back at Christmas and loaded my one year's worth of luggage into a rented car.

I drove south, collecting the air and the sun. To La Mancha, the red birthmark on the belly of Spain.

In the town of Consuegra it was siesta. I was the only one on the streets, left to cool alone. I climbed the stone stairway to the hill of windmills and gazed up at their improbability, wondering about my own desire to let my skirts fly just one last time.

Then on to Valdepeñas, where I wanted to stay, forget Sevilla, and live in the valley of rocks where houses slip into the hills without a sound. Where I wanted to shop in the all-white tile market for fresh figs and fish and sit forever in the plaza alongside the fountain, its water-washed tiles blazing.

But my destination was Sevilla, the flamenco of the Gypsies, and Pio.

I was nervous about meeting Pio. I imagined his studio with clean white walls and shining mirrors. Pio, himself, sleek and well-dressed; Aurora, his wife, svelte, wearing fine jewelry. Both of them living with chrome and black wood.

In northern California, I had met Rosario, Pio's younger brother, seen him perform in San Francisco. Cradling his guitar like a beloved, rocking it back and forth, he revealed himself, dark and light. And he revealed Sevilla, its gold and lace history, its thievery.

Rosario wandered in a field of feelings: his joy left an edge of gold around his religion. In his pain, the long-dead reappeared. He sang while he played; his song raw, it tasted of the olive-saturated earth of Spain.

In his hands, the guitar could be laughter. Or a hollow sound where only pain belonged. He had the *duende*—a mysterious power, Goethe said, that all may feel and nobody can explain. But everybody tries. Except the Gypsies. Neither Rosario nor Pio nor any of the Gypsies I was to meet ever mentioned the word. For them the *duende* was a given, not a goal.

I looked on their art with enormous eyes. But I had no expectations that I could do it. Rosario, however, left an impression—a big gap—between what he did and the stale bread of theatrical flamenco I had been performing for five years.

A few weeks later, I bumped into him on the street, learned he had an apartment not far from where I lived. And *yes,* he taught the dance.

~

Connecting with Rosario, intending only a taste of his flamenco, his *duende* met me halfway, took me by the hand and led me to where I had always wanted to be. In a very short time, I was in his world wholeheartedly.

He taught the entire art of flamenco: guitar, *cante*, and dance in his 'studio,' a basement apartment so small he had to stand wedged in a corner in order to teach. The dance space was a four by eight plywood board. While Rosario played, sang, and stabbed a stick into the floor, I turned a tight curl at each end of the board and danced back and forth like a bird on a perch.

I studied each new step of his in a rapture. I was out of my normal mind; the music and the heelwork wound themselves around me; I heard nothing else.

But Rosario wasn't a dancer. He couldn't help me find the place where my body belonged. I had been told in theatrical flamenco to 'dance tall,' with almost straight knees. And here I was trying to find the earth. And after all my years as a ballet dancer, soft-footed and quiet, the flamenco heelwork eluded me.

He said, often, that he had learned all he knew of the dance from watching Pio.

Rosario told me all about Pio: he was the last of his line from the Golden Age of flamenco; he had been a great dancer; now he was a great choreographer, and a master teacher. But Pio was getting old; he wasn't well; he wouldn't be teaching much longer. "Doloré," Rosario would say, "You've got to get to Sevilla. You've got to study with Pio!" But get to Spain? My hope was the size of a mustard seed.

It all came together, however, through the shadow end of life: my dog, fourteen years old, that I couldn't leave behind, died; and I got laid off my job.

So even knowing I would be returning to the States fifty-six years old with no work, I took what money I had, and I went to Spain.

Rosario encouraged me: "And when you get to Sevilla, Doloré, I will come. I will come and I will help you with Pio's choreography. Because it is hard, very hard. And I will introduce you to the real flamencos, Doloré, the *puros!*"

~

After driving all day from Madrid, I arrived in Sevilla spent. I turned in my car to the garage under the Alfonso Trece Hotel, went upstairs for one long look at the interior courtyard, the cut-out Islamic windows, the palm trees and fading sun, the dinner being served to a chamber music concert. I sighed and took a taxi to the Barrio Santa Cruz in the "Designated Tourist Zone." The *barrio*, all dappled light by day. By night, a golden maze.

I took the first *pensión* I saw. Pretty enough on the outside, all tiles and arches. Inside, my room had only cold water; I could count the springs under the mattress; I had to cross an open rooftop to get to the bathroom.

In the morning, I left the peeling wallpaper of my room to seek out Pio. I walked past the Cathedral stabbing at the sky, past the Giralda, that chunky, straight-up tower with balconies about to fall over, through the street of antique dealers, past the sixteenth century City Jail where Cervantes, aging and impoverished, wrote *Don Quixote*, to Sierpes.

Sierpes is a serpentine walking street. It is narrow, just wide enough for beggars to walk on their knees, eyes lowered, arms outstretched carrying homemade banners: "no money, no job, no food."

Sierpes is neon signs, old banks, men's clubs, slits for bars. And stores for everything.

I stopped to look at the shoes that wrap the foot with the fine leathers of Spain, the stores for machine-made castanets and hand-embroidered shawls, the magazine kiosks, the bookstore with secret spaces for all-day browsing, the stalls for bullfight tickets, the art supply stores, and the sweet shop that sells *yemas,* the egg yolk and sugar candy that dissolves teeth.

At the end of Sierpes, I crossed the big boulevard to the 'other' Sevilla, the Gypsy *barrio.* Its narrow winding streets— starting, stopping, curving, backtracking—changed their names at every intersection. The whole *barrio* was a big secret.

In the melon morning, the women with their string shopping bags left footprints of light on the washed-down sidewalks. I followed them under balconies of bougainvillea and geraniums to where the hot noose of darkness was hidden—where Pio and Aurora Mendoza lived.

I was looking for #12 Espiritu Santo. I finally found it and rang at a very white house with bright yellow trim. A little woman looked out of her door and wagged her head in the direction of an apartment building half a block away.

There is no East, West, North, or South Espiritu Santo. But two #12s. Four doors from the white house, in the dark, fish-smelling foyer of a shabby apartment building, I buzzed a buzzer.

Nothing happened. Another little woman stuck her head out of a first-floor door and said, "Yell."

I yelled. On the second floor a door opened, then slammed.

My eyes still blinking from the sun, I saw only a form step to the head of the stairs. It filled the space between the banisters and made a loud, rhythmic, blowing noise.

Then I saw a face, narrow at the forehead, the eyes small, the nose spread out, the balloon cheeks sliding down into a wide neck. Under a print dress, covered by a dirty apron, sheet-size, an enormous bosom and belly were all one.

It was Aurora. Three hundred pounds.

She came down the steps heavy, breathing aloud, puffing white spots on her cheeks.

At the bottom of the stairs, she looked up at me with her close-set eyes. I talked to them, "My name is Doloré."

Her eyes didn't move. My words seemed stuck in the air.

I tried again. This time, the lace cuff of Madrid: It would give me great pleasure if you would permit me to introduce myself.

Nothing.

I tried again. I wanted to study with Pio, I said.

At that Aurora blinked. She made a sound like small pebbles rolling downhill.

"Eh?" I asked.

But Pio Mateo Mendoza, who had been listening on the landing, got the point that I was a new student. He pounded down the stairs. At the bottom, he snapped words at Aurora, who grunted, turned, and pulled herself back up to the landing, one step at a time.

Pio, half a head shorter than I was, a scrawny, brassy little man in soiled and crumpled clothes, stood at the bottom of the stairs and smiled all his teeth up at me.

In that moment, my imaginings collided with reality; my hopes sank out the bottoms of my shoes. I was reeling with disappointment.

But Pio, oblivious to my feelings, linked his arm in mine and took me at once to see his studio.

• 2 •

ALEGRÍAS

Stepping for the first time from the bright white of the street into the darkness of Pio's studio, I smelled stale cigarette butts, sweat, dust, and red wine.

Pio flicked on the fluorescent lights. The walls of the studio were sudden.

His *academía* was no more than a smoky, dingy room. The dance space had a splintery wooden floor so small I would be dancing on the head of a pin. There was no air; the only window was tightly shut. The bar at one end of the studio was strewn with empty wine bottles. On the floor there were overflowing ashtrays, trash in the corners, and old newspapers.

I wondered if anything good could come out of Pio's studio. I wondered what the hell I was doing there.

But I hadn't wanted to study in Madrid where flamenco is danced by pretty girls, their arms pinned in place, hands clacking out the castanets. There is no time for undulating hips or feet churning the dirt.

And certainly, no time for flamenco as a way of life.

In Sevilla, flamenco starts up on street corners or in bars, with a couple of guitarists, a singer, a dancer. It is men and women sitting at night on wooden chairs on the sidewalk, clapping the rhythms. In mom and pop markets, old men sing their grocery lists. Little girls, their arms writhing like baby snakes, dance the

9

Sevillanas by the river. At Christmas time, "Oh Come All Ye Faithful" has a flamenco beat.

Flamenco classes in Madrid were regimented, well-organized, all taught in a building on a street named *Amor de Dios,* "The Love of God."

Flamenco lessons in Sevilla were catch-as-catch-can. My friend Mimi studied with Carmencita. Mimi tracked her down to her apartment, found her in the bathroom, and took her lessons there. Mario Esteban Alvarez taught in a garage with wavy floors and grease in the air. Amparo Garcia taught somewhere outside of Sevilla in a barn by a stream with no address.

The grand old masters of flamenco, El Cojo and Realito, were gone, doors closed, studios boarded up. Only Pio, all flint and stone, hung on. His *academía* was the shabby, unimportant place where everyone finally came to study.

So I started with old Pio and coped with him on a daily basis.

~

The only things that started on time in Sevilla were the bullfights and Pio's lessons—ten a.m. every morning, *en punto.*

I left my apartment at 9:55, as late as I dared; I wanted to avoid conversation with Pio. I wasn't usually successful.

He would grab me by the elbow as soon as I entered the studio, point to to a poster of himself as a young dancer, hands on his hips, thick black curls at his neck, and intone his name, *THE PHENOMENAL PIO MATEO MENDOZA.* "And here I am at the Royal Theatre in Madrid. I was the headliner!" He could spend twenty minutes of my precious hour talking about himself.

Also in the mornings, he left the big double doors to the studio open. Men would drift into his studio smoking, talking, helping themselves to a glass of red wine from his bar. Pio would turn from me to them and say, "Do you remember me in the *Bulerías*?" Then he'd demonstrate a step, always the same step. They'd nod, drink, and go on talking.

These were the men who hung around all day on the streets of Pio's *barrio*, marked by a shadow around its edges. This is where the yellow and white world of Sevilla stops and the color gray becomes streets and buildings. Where the light is darker and it is old light. The *barrio* of the outcasts: the unknown bullfighters, the Gypsies, and the flamencos.

There was the hunchback with the lantern jaw and yellow teeth who never shaved but never grew a beard. Another man who sold lottery tickets off the back of his wrists because his hands hung down soft and useless. The *cojo*, the crippled ex-bullfighter, who slept in the doorway of my apartment building with a bottle for a pillow. Old Tomás, a dried leaf of a man, walked all day from bar to bar to sing for his drinks in whispers.

I was glad the men came in the studio. They circulated the air a bit and gave me my chance to get away from the photographs on Pio's wall, and start dancing by myself. The sound of heelwork would eventually attract Pio's attention. Better yet, I would make a mistake.

Pio loved it when I made mistakes; he would slam his cane to the floor and bellow, "No!" Then take my arm and show me the step, his trousers flapping around his skinny legs.

Once I got his attention, he was be glued to my exertion. There would be nothing between me and his will.

~

During the time I was with Pio, students came to him from Japan, France, Germany, England, even Russia. But when I first started with him, he had just reopened his studio after a year in the

11

hospital, and he had only a boy from Córdoba, a red-headed woman from Sevilla, two of his nieces whose names he could never remember, and Kimiko, the tall Japanese girl. And myself. Alone. Pio taught only private lessons. He stood in the center of his studio like a ringmaster at a circus, while around and around the little studio I went, holding my long skirt off the floor with both hands, doing Pio's heelwork exercises, and feeling my legs fall off.

For the first two weeks with Pio, I did nothing else. He pounded his cane and called the counts. If I slowed down in the exercises, he yelled, "*Rápida, rápida, más rápida.*" If I had trouble turning a corner, he yelled, "*Rápida, rápida, más rápida.*" If I stayed in one spot, he yelled, "*Rápida, rápida, más rápida.*"

My sweat came out of the walls.

But at the end of my two weeks' initiation, I could charge up my unthinking heels, pick them up and put them down on the right dime, move out faster and faster. My heelwork became a texture of sound. Not a machine gun, but musical, lace patterns laid out on the floor in birds, leaves, lovers, and Gypsy stories.

Pio then pronounced me ready to learn the *Alegrías*, the most joyous dance in the flamenco repertoire.

~

There are many types of joy. There is the full-blown sort, bursting out in overbearing laughter; there is the silent, inside joy that glows in the darkness. There is also a giggle in the soul, for no one but one's self.

And there is Gypsy joy.

Pio, in pain, no money, no self-respect, sad behind the eyes, could still dance the *Alegrías* with a spark of light going up his spine and out his smile.

At night in the bars, he danced in small, tight spaces the

width of his own body. But his heelwork went clear down to the center of the earth.

Other bodies stood close to his, breathed the same air, let his energy fire up the night for them. He became big in their moment, connecting them to the joy in themselves.

~

I learned the *Alegrías* by imitating Pio.

Pio's knees and elbows bent like broken matchsticks; his dance was angular, taut.

But he could imitate the woman's dance, the coiling movement of the female body, her hips rolling, arms wrapping her torso, her fingers calling the night birds from the trees.

He used his shirttails to teach me on which hip to hold my heavy skirt, switching it quickly from side to side. How to kick it high with my knees so the ruffled petticoats showed, then catch it in the air with two fingers.

He stood beside me, his hand cupping my elbow, as I followed his heelwork. Like a horse picking up speed, from gait to gait to gallop. The sharp thrust of accents broke the rhythms into fresh patterns. Oh, so difficult to copy.

But Pio could be the soul of patience. "Doloré, listen. Watch me. No, use the other foot for that accent. Trust me." I trusted him and found the sudden syncopated hiccups that moved me into a joyous counterpoint with the guitar. The long-repeated passages of the heelwork became as intricate as the winding streets of Sevilla. I'd get lost. "Pio...I can't remember."

"That's all right, Doloré. From the beginning—again."

At the end of the heelwork section, the rhythms came faster, like blood racing. Then suddenly—the cessation of all sound. Except a single heel beating out the life pulse.

The lyrical section, the *silencio*, of the *Alegrías* was next. Pio would hum the melody, *"Ta...ta...ta...."* I would follow him as he moved diagonally, quietly; we were sidewinders without our rattles.

He would measure out the distances, so much for this step, so much for that. "Doloré, curl the end of the *silencio*," he'd say, "like a cat's tail."

I followed Pio in the perfect emptiness, the next move, like the next thought, always unknown. I copied his steps, pouring all my energy into them, as if they were my last drink of water.

When Pio finished teaching me his *Alegrías*, he pronounced it "great," and himself, "genius."

~

It took the whole month of July just to learn Pio's steps. And a little bit about Pio, himself.

Sometime during every lesson, he would wander back to the wall of his youth. "There. In that photograph, Doloré. There I am." He'd stand looking up at the pictures, tracing the big scar on his left temple gently with his middle finger, feeling the new geography of his body.

Then he'd turn to me. "This cost me a year in the hospital," he'd say. "At the fair I got kicked in the head. By a horse."

The scar was a perfect horseshoe in shape and size. I didn't doubt his story.

Not yet I didn't.

• 3 •

LOS FLAMENCOS

July, I learned the *Alegrías*; August, I practiced it.

Temperatures were rising to 110° on the street. My flamenco skirt, fifteen yards of fabric, could stand up by itself from dried sweat.

Pio smoked between yelling at me.

When I could no longer breathe, I'd swing the big double doors by their brass knobs to catch what air I could from the street. This alarmed Pio because the door hinges, like everything else in the old *barrio*, were falling apart. He conceded, finally, it was hot. He bought a small electric fan—complaining to me about the expense.

Heat didn't matter to Pio. He wanted me to dance the *Alegrías* at breakneck speed; he wanted me to develop strength. These things mattered. He'd say, "You will dance one hour, Doloré. I will build you to one hour of dancing, one hour straight, no breaks, no breaths."

Every morning, I practiced the *Alegrías* over and over, Pio's cane demanding an edge more of speed, of precision, until my heels became running beads of sound, clear as drops of water on glass.

But Pio didn't always have the stamina to teach. He was thin, his arms hanging out of his short sleeves like hairy twigs. He'd suddenly tire and sit down, forgetting what he had just told me to do.

It would be Joselito then who would help me out.

Joselito came into the studio every day. A tall, skinny man, he had to fold himself in half to squeeze in the little chairs lining the studio. He'd sit watching every lesson with his long legs crossed, his chin almost resting on his knees.

When I didn't understand Pio, Joselito would point out the direction I should move with little finger-tappings on the air. Or he'd rap out a difficult rhythm on his kneecap with his knuckles.

Joselito was the ultimate *aficionado*. He collected the careers of the great flamencos, held them in memory. He spent hours in the bars arguing over details, refining each bit of information, allowing nothing and no one to be forgotten. For him, no master of the art had ever died. And he dedicated himself to Pio.

But he didn't get any thanks for helping Pio's students—or for keeping Pio out of scrapes. Just out of the hospital, Pio would become disoriented on the street; Joselito followed him anytime he left the studio.

I was in the shoe repair shop the day Pio entered, Joselito right behind him.

I was a regular at the shoemaker's. I came to Spain with one pair of Gallardo's flamenco shoes—red—and made them last. When I left, the inner soles had been replaced twice, the heels re-glued, the nails pounded back in the tips, the elastic straps tightened, and the big holes over the little toes patched.

I was sitting, waiting for my shoes, when Pio entered, walked up to the customer's counter—and asked for a beer.

Joselito stepped up to him and spoke quietly, "Pio, this isn't a bar."

Pio replied in full voice, "Then—what is it?"

"It's the shoemaker's."

Pio snapped, "What's it doing here? This is where the Bar Alonzo is."

"No, Pio, it's—"

"I've lived in this *barrio* forty years! Don't you think I know where the Bar Alonzo is?"

The men at the machines put down the shoes, sat back in their chairs, picked up their cigarettes, and stared at Pio who stared back at them. "A beer!" he demanded. "What's the matter? You don't understand? You don't think I can pay?" He fished in his pockets—and came up empty. His voice softened; he smiled, "But you all know me. You know I'm good for it."

"Pio, this is the shoemaker's," Joselito repeated.

Pio put his nose up to Joselito's chin and said, "Then you idiot! What did you bring me in here for?"

Without waiting for an answer, Pio turned and stomped out of the shop, snarling back over his shoulder at Joselito, "What'sa matter? You don't think I know where I'm going?"

Where he was 'going' was always to another bar.

There were eight bars in a two-block radius of his studio. Since he never paid back a dime of credit, he wasn't welcome in any of them.

That didn't stop him from trying.

Bar Siete Puertas is the oldest in Sevilla; it has seven doors open to the street. Pio would go in one and be smoothly ushered out the next.

Other bars wouldn't be so smooth. He'd be hustled out bodily, yelling, "You don't understand. I'm Pio Mateo Mendoza! What's money compared to my talent?"

But Pio could get into the Bar Casa Calixto; he was small and it was big. Without being seen by the barmen, he could make his way like a beetle through the bunches of Spaniards standing with their drinks. Then he'd quickly sit down at a table and join in on the *tertulias.*

The *tertulias* are for drinking and talking. The Spanish men with flaccid faces, all their features drooping, sit at round tables and talk by the hour: the Madrileños cynically view themselves and their city; the Sevillanos declare repeatedly that Sevilla is the divine earth of Spain; they talk the religion of the bull, and flamenco.

Over their wine glasses, they compare the old singers to the current singers. They remember a single word of a single song; they discuss *duende*, who has it, and who hasn't.

Opinions around the table differ. But the rule of pleasantness always holds.

Except with Pio. He was not wanted; he made excuses when it was his turn to buy a round. And Pio wasn't jovial. His talk was self-centered, loud, and contentious.

By way of the web of gossip in Sevilla, I heard about Pio and the *tertulias.* "La Niña," he'd say in his gravel voice, his big fig nose bobbing up and down with every word, "was the best singer ever. *Gitana Pura!*"

"Uh, Pio," the man with the tousled hair and knock-kneed eyes would respond, "everybody knows she wasn't Gypsy."

"She had to be. Nobody but a Gypsy could sing like that. Flamenco is pure Gypsy!"

"Uh, Pio, flamenco, it isn't Gypsy. It's Andalu."

"Pio," another man would interject, "flamenco was here before you Gypsies arrived."

"No! We brought flamenco to Spain!"

"Pio, it's great art what you do, but—"

"*Sí.* Everybody knows—I was the best dancer. Now I am the best teacher."

"But you Gypsies borrowed from what you saw here."

"Spaniards!" Pio's words like a battering ram. "You stole flamenco from us. And now you claim it was yours all along!"

"Pio, nobody stole flamenco from you."

"*Hombre!* Now you're saying it's only the Gypsies who steal!"

The Spanish men, holding their manners like cards in their hands, say nothing. They communicate only with their eyes: "Who let him in?" Then they get up all together, at once, leaving Pio alone at the table.

But he always came back to the *tertulias*. Over a glass of wine he could pull out the fine threads of memory and look at each one with a small breath of interest. He could remember the old days with a few oldish men.

~

The controversy over the origins of flamenco has never been settled.

I asked Pio one morning about mid-eastern influences in flamenco. He was staring up at his photographs; my voice startled him. His shoulders bounced once, "Huh, Doloré?"

"Flamenco, Pio, there's belly dance in it."

"No. It's pure Gypsy."

"But Pio—"

"Doloré, if you already know, why are you asking me? I tell you, flamenco came from the Gypsies...where else? We were first."

"First, Pio?"

"*Sí*, Doloré. We were the first people, the royal people. God created us first. We were first in the Bible and we will be first in Heaven. And we brought music into the world. Without us, there would be no music. And no flamenco."

"If you say so, Pio."

~

In August, I pleased Pio; I danced well. He was always the first to congratulate himself, "I told you, Doloré, I told you I was a good teacher!"

Also in August, he took me on a 'field trip' through his *barrio*.

I was already familiar with the big conservatory of music, serious and well-organized (for Sevilla). And the conservatory of dance, beautiful studios—but no flamenco allowed. The *Academía* of Zarzuela, where little girls from 'good' families belted out the bright songs of turn-of-the-century Madrid.

I had watched young boys practicing bullfight passes on the sidewalks with kitchen knives for horns and capes the size of bed sheets. While littler boys, practicing for *Semana Santa*, Holy Week, marched through the streets with bugles and flutes, banging on drums like pots.

But Pio had things he wanted to show me himself. He knew the history of his *barrio*. He had known all the old flamencos and whatever rabbit holes they had lived in. He took me into the alleyways behind the alleys.

The *barrio* used to be pockmarked with one-room apartments and small bars and cafés where the flamencos sat and sang all day.

He showed me the room where Manuel Torre, the consummate *Siguiriyas* singer, died in poverty, his only possessions a greyhound dog and a fighting rooster.

We saw the boarded-up studio of Enrique, *El Cojo*, who limped when he walked, but not when he danced.

The shop of Silverio, the tailor, a part-time bullfighter. He was the first to sing flamenco in public.

The studio of the guitarist, Paco Lucena, who always broke his new guitars because he said they sounded better after they were repaired.

Pio showed me the sagging balconies, no longer in use, where the old flamencos sang *Saetas,* ecstatic love arrows, to the statue of the Virgin as she was carried through the *barrio*: "*Aiii...* My beloved. Flame of living love! You wound me in the center of my soul!"

I asked him about a big shiny plaque hanging outside of a building, half torn down. The tiles announced the *Academía Realito.* "It was the studio of Miguel Real, Doloré. *El Realito,* he was called."

"The studio, Pio, it's all closed up?"

"Oh, *sí,* Doloré. *Hace mucho tiempo*, a long time ago. But the old man, he still used to come and sit in the Alameda and tell everybody how it was—who was a good dancer and who wasn't. He knew I was the best."

"If you say so, Pio."

We stopped in the café where Lorca sat and wrote. Under his photograph we had good madeleines and great coffee (I bought). "Doloré," Pio said over his coffee, "Lorca, he used to live in this *barrio*. He'd sit in a corner and write while the flamencos sang. And look, Doloré," Pio pointed out the window, "that's the Alameda de Hercules. Lorca, himself, declaimed there!"

Across the street was a dusty strip of bare land. I had seen it before; nothing to look at—no trees, no grass, no use—except for flea markets.

Staring out the window, Pio said. "It's all gone, now. But there used to be performances, Doloré. Three stages set up every night. The greatest flamencos, singers, dancers, guitarists. They all came here to perform!"

When we finished our coffee, we walked across the intersection and into the Alameda.

Pio stopped and stood in front of the statue of a woman, her shoulders wrapped in a shawl, hands on her hips. Looking up at her he said, "This was Pastora Pavón, Doloré. *La Niña*, we called her. She was the best singer ever!"

As we were talking, a woman with a string bag of groceries passed by us. "Pio," she said, "your woman is looking for you." Without a word to me, Pio turned and ran off.

And I was left standing where the great flamenco singers had filled the air with the sound of seabirds, and cracked dry land. Where they had performed night after night as if nothing would ever change, as if no war could ever touch the Alameda de Hercules.

· 4 ·

LA ALAMEDA DE HERCULES

The Alameda is now only a shadow of joy, a nothing strip of gray land between the pedestals of heroes where, after dark, prostitutes in see-through body stockings call the men from the taxis. But the ghosts of Sevilla get out of bed and walk the Alameda de Hercules, trailing their memories behind them.

When Sevilla was a glow on the map, lace was a way of life. Horses danced their carriages through the streets; white doves, their wings whirring in the air, landed in clusters in the Alameda, and rose again at one word, a canopy of white. The Spaniards promenaded as if nothing were happening. The extraordinary was ordinary; life was threaded through the needle of becoming.

By night, under paper lanterns strung from tree to tree, the Gypsies sang for the Spaniards who sat on the grass and listened to the Gypsy voices open the canister of night, letting out bats and owls.

Afterwards, the Gypsies crossed the street to their communal *vecindades*. In the cobbled patios with climbing bougainvillea and running rats, they sat singing in a circle until morning.

One woman, Pastora Pavón, held the community together, although she wasn't a Gypsy. They called her the Lady of The Combs for the tortoise combs that held her hair. When she died she took the last of the Alameda with her. The Gypsies left. The old *vecindades* were torn down to make room for empty lots.

~

Pastora Pavón, when she was old, sang the *Alegrías* low between the shreds of her voice.

But when she sang the *Siguiriyas,* she bellowed, frightening the birds from the trees.

She sat and sang every day under a tree, spreading her skirts and *montoncillo* out in the shade 'til its fringe reached the edge of the shadow. The Gypsies adored her. They brought her buttered toast and red wine. She held their babies on her big lap.

Aficionados who couldn't sing, but could feel, came to sit with her and listen.

Some stayed to hear her flick the rhythms off the end of her tongue.

Many left, having come for the 'real' flamenco. Having gotten it, they left to meet over candles and talk about flamenco. She laughed at them. She believed only in the Gypsies.

It was Joselito who told me about Pastora and Pio.

Joselito loved Sevilla. He coddled the old city, the Moors' beehive of streets where outstretched fingertips could touch both sides at once, of empty patios enclosed by sighs. He knew the history of the small daisy city. He could kick a rock in any street and tell me who had lived there, whose carriage had passed that way to the Maestranza Bullring. Who had died when, in what room.

I sat and talked with Joselito one day during my lesson.

Pio had run out of the studio to the nearest friendly bar for a beer. I timed him once. He could run the block and a half, swallow the beer straight down and return—all in five minutes.

This day he took fifteen minutes. Three beers.

Sitting in my long skirt, sweaty around the waist, my shoes off, I sat with my head close to Joselito's to catch his soft words

24

with the smeared endings.

"*Eh*, I remember, Doloré. When I was a kid. Pastora, she was the greatest of the flamenco *cantaos**. And the flamencos then, you understand, they were bullfighters and singers and dancers and guitarists and poets. Lorca, he was a flamenco. All of them, their blood moved to the *compás*. They all lived here, in this *barrio*. Pio, you know, he was a kid, maybe fourteen, when he came to Sevilla, skinny as a stick and with pimples. But he was *gitano puro;* he knew who Pastora was."

"Joselito," I said, "I remember what Pio told me when I first started with him, how he came to Sevilla and went straight to Pastora and said, 'Watch me. I'll be famous one day.'"

"*Sí.*" Joselito went on, "He found her in the Alameda his first day in Sevilla and walked right past all the *aficionaos** sitting on the grass, and said, 'If you'll sing for me, I'll dance for you.' And Pastora, she looked him up and down and smiled and said, 'Who the hell are you?'"

Joselito laughed and recrossed his legs and went on, "So Pio, he told her his name and where he came from and all about his *mare** and *pare**. Then he said, 'And someday I'll be a famous dancer. And you have the opportunity right now to help me.' Pastora, she laughed 'til all her back teeth showed. 'Did you hear him?' she said to the *aficionaos*. 'Did you hear? This kid, from nowhere. He's telling me, Pastora Pavón, what I should do for him!' But then she turned to Pio, 'All right. Go ahead and dance. I've seen all you kids. And you all stink. But go ahead anyway. I'll sing for you, but only because you're Gypsy.'"

"Then did Pio dance for her?" I asked. "On the spot?"

---

* Andalus pronunciation.

"Oh, Pio danced, Doloré. And when he finished, she said to

him, right in front of all the *aficionaos*, and they all agreed with her, of course, she said straight to Pio, `You stink.' Well, Pio, he got red in the face and spat at her feet and yelled at her, `I'm the best thing you've ever seen. And the fastest. And if you're too dumb to see that, I'll find someone smarter!' Pastora, she swore, `*Hijo de Puta!* You stinking little bastard. Get out of my sight!' And she yelled to the *aficionaos*, `Get him out of here!' So two of the *aficionaos*, they stood up and put hands on Pio. Well, they were sorry. 'Cause he flattened them on the spot. And the others ran.

"When Pastora saw the *aficionaos* out cold on the grass and Pio red in the face and breathing like a bull, she shook her head and laughed, *'Mare de Dios!* You've got guts. So you want me to help you? Then you go dance in the streets for a year, a whole year. Like *Escudero*. Like all the others. And if you can do that, then come back and see me. Then on my word, I'll help you.'"

Joselito stopped talking to light a new cigarette from the butt of his old one. Shifting in my chair, feeling my legs getting cold, I urged him on: "So, tell me—what did Pio do?"

"Oh, he left and went to Sierpes by the candy store not far from the magazine kiosk. And he danced there every day, for pennies, and how he slept in the back of a bar on boxes, and it wasn't often he had enough to eat."

"Pio," I added, "told me a little bit about dodging the police, and the *gente* with the shell games who tried to run him off."

"*Sí,* Doloré. But one day, and Pio had been dancing there almost a year, Pastora took a walk down Sierpes. Now Pastora, she never took a walk on Sierpes. But that day she did—with all the *aficionaos* following her. They followed her, you know, like she was a bullfighter, everywhere. And they'd say to each other, `Have you heard La Pastora sing the *Soleá*, she sings it like two angels!' They'd say it loud so everybody on the street would know they knew Pastora. Anyway, there was Pio dancing. And she stopped and sang the *Alegrías* for him and clapped the *compás*."

"But tell me, Joselito," I interrupted, "what did he dance like?"

"Pio told me he never danced better in his life than he did that day for Pastora. I wasn't there but I heard he was a *monstruo*— so fast his feet blurred. And the *aficionaos*, they all thought Pio must be famous 'cause Pastora was singing for him. So they said to him, `Come with us and we'll buy you a drink.'"

"I'm betting they took Pio and Pastora to that big bar behind the bullring."

"*Sí,* and all the way over, Pio walked alongside Pastora like he was her equal. And Pastora giggled 'cause she thought it was a good joke on the *aficionaos*. Well, when they got inside the big bar, Pio sat himself down at the head of the long table right next to Pastora and he ate better than he had in a month. Then one of the *aficionaos* said, `Señor Pio, where do you dance next?' Pio, he looked straight at Pastora and he said, `Ask her. She's my agent.' And all the heads turned at the same click and looked at her. Pastora, she was taken by surprise. But she said, `Well, Madrid, Barcelona, then maybe Paris.' That was how Pio got started."

"So what did Pastora actually do for Pio?"

"Pastora, she was a woman of honor, Doloré. 'Cause she said it, she did it. She got Pio in with some flamencos going to Madrid. Then later he went to Paris and even London. And the audiences, they loved him 'cause he was a kid and his legs snapped like scissors. He was, like he said, the fastest thing they had ever seen. But none of the flamencos liked him. He was a *presumío*. He thought he was better than all of them and he told them so. Pastora, though, she adored him. Every time Pio came back to Sevilla to perform, she'd sing for him. Where she wouldn't for any of the other dancers. And she told everybody that she had discovered Pio, and she spotted his talent at once."

Joselito laughed again, put out his cigarette, and said, "Pio, he got famous 'cause of Pastora."

• 5 •

DON DINERO

Sevilla had always been Pio's favorite city to perform in. After performances, before dawn, when even Sevilla was asleep, he would go down to the river. Still in his flamenco boots, he'd rattle out rhythms on the quay, his heels heard only by the inner ear of sleepers. Dancing alone, he needed no applause, no reassurance that he was a master.

Alone, he'd dance out what he hadn't dared on the stage, rhythms the guitarists didn't foresee or couldn't follow.

Pio could step on any stage and match his heels to the rhythms he heard around him: the click of a guitarist's fingernails, the jingle of jewelry, an insect buzzing a light, the beat of silence.

As a teacher, Pio rarely spoke about his ability to do this; he knew it was a gift. He couldn't explain it; he didn't expect the same from his students.

For us, he had to trap a rhythm, repeating it over and over with his own heels. Until, tamed and compliant, it was ours to accomplish, and remember.

His rhythms were his cherished children. He never forgot even one of them. He could recall rhythms from fifteen years before. "This is an old one, Doloré," he would say, his voice cooing. "No one knows it but me. And now, *mi alma,* I'm giving it to you. Where are you ever going to find a better teacher?"

These were the times I could have hugged Pio. There would

29

be just that dot of land that told me he knew I was there. It happened only once in a while; I regret I could never be close to him.

But what I came to Spain for, I got. It was in his dusty, dirty studio that the *compás*, the driving energy, and the gutsy Gypsy line, all came into my body.

Teaching intensely, choreographing quickly and easily, Pio would remind me on a daily basis how lucky I was to be studying with him. He'd yell at each new step, "I'm the best!" As a teacher he was almost as good as he said he was. And generous: he shared his mastery with his students.

Pio *sí mismo*, Pio himself, was a different story. My clearest mental picture of him is with his hand out, palm up. Dealing with Pio and money was sliding on ice.

I suspected that he was keeping me going on the *Alegrías* longer than necessary, putting off starting the *Siguiriyas* for the money. It wouldn't have been out of character.

But Pio was no different than many of his clan. The Gypsies were my friends; I had been in their homes, sat their children on my lap, cooked with the women, listened to their life stories. But when it came to money, I was always on the outside. The hands which held mine could also hold knives. The unexpected cold turn the Gypsies could take never ceased to shock me. It was like banging into a glass door.

~

Over time, I learned the Gypsies' many attitudes to money, those with sunken faces and thin, oily braids who stole at flea markets. The Gypsies who wouldn't work for any man, who sold junk out of donkey carts and lived in cardboard shacks. The Gypsies who eschewed money altogether. They had left even the cardboard shacks. They lived under bridges in ankle-deep water with their cows and goats.

There were others, still more difficult to understand: the young Gypsy mother who sat on Sierpes and begged, a baby rolling in her big belly. She was sixteen and already had two small, fragile children with crooked limbs, eyes dirty from crying, beside her. Never looking higher than the knees of the pedestrians, the mother sat on a blanket all day taking money. At night, she and the children went home to a rag house. The family ate around a three-legged card table. There was an old stove in a corner with a big enamel coffee pot on it. The pot was never used because it was stuffed with money.

Then there were the *canasteros* who still traveled. Wooden wagons had become aluminum trailers pulled by late-model American cars. Horse-trading and fortune-telling were replaced by drug-dealing.

Pio's clan were *caseros*; they no longer traveled; they no longer lived in caves. They lived in flats and houses. And they wanted the things money could buy.

For Pio, money put in his hands by another was the measure of his worth. Pio often said of himself, "I was rich. Now I am poor. I have no money to prove who I was. Or who I am."

Disbelieving, shaking his head, he would say over and over, *"La vida, la vida."* Life. It had come down hard on Pio. All his art reduced to one shabby little studio. Before the hospital, he had had three studios, all thriving. While he was in the hospital, his family managed to keep up the rent only on the smallest—on Matamoros—and he returned to it anonymous.

Pio had numerous schemes, subtle and not so subtle, for separating me from my money. I learned early the big cut he was taking for himself, for tickets to a special flamenco performance, for handmade laces from the lace shop, for the woman who made flamenco costumes. He was only too willing to take me around. It took me a little longer to realize he was making a tip on each sale, the cost being passed on to me.

On the other hand, Pio didn't see why he had to pay for anything. His response to being thrown out of a bar was, "Just because I owe them money. What is money compared to my talent?"

Bills received in the mail especially provoked him. "Don't they know who I am?" he'd say.

The mailman came into the studio every day during my lesson. He'd walk across the dance space never looking up from his envelopes. I danced beside him, around him, and past him; I sprayed sweat on his shoes. But we never collided.

Pio would share his mail with me, "Look. Look, Doloré. All these people are writing me!" His 'mail' was advertising flyers. Pio treated every ad for house cleaning, auto painting, new *sombrillas*, vacations to Mallorca or Marbella, as personal correspondence. "Look. Look at the envelope, Doloré. They're writing to me! They know my address. They want me to take a trip to Málaga. They're giving me a special rate. They want me to enjoy the beach. Don't they know I don't like the beach? Well, they forgot."

But the bills got wadded up and tossed in the top drawer of an old bureau that served for his desk. They were never seen again except when he would take one out, one with red print, and wave it in my face while I was dancing. "I'm closing the studio," he'd announce as he jogged in front of me.

I'd stop, "What?"

"They're coming tomorrow," he'd say, and wave the bill close enough so I could feel the breeze, but not close enough so I could see the print. "They're coming—to turn it off."

"Pio! Turn off what?"

"The electricity."

"Who is?"

"They are."

"Why?"

"'Cause you don't pay me enough, Doloré. I can't pay my bills. So, I have to close the studio."

"Pio. I've paid you in advance!"

"So you give me another advance, Doloré. Then you'll be paid up to the end of next month. Won't that be wonderful?"

~

Pio had returned to teaching unknown and with few students. It wasn't long, however, before word got out. Within a month after I started with him, his schedule was as tight as his fist; he was teaching from ten in the morning until eight at night.

As he began getting new students, he composed a syllogism: "I'm the best flamenco teacher in Spain. Students are coming to me from all over the world—France, Germany, America, Japan. So, I'm the best teacher in the whole world!"

Which was sufficient justification for raising his tuition. The day he did it, Pio didn't ask, or explain. He yelled—from across the studio, "You have to pay. You must!"

He bellowed like a bull. While I fried my mind trying to guess how much more he wanted, what this would do to my budget, and who else I could study from.

He named a figure twice what I was paying.

When I told him I had to think it over, he yelled back, who was I to argue with him, and didn't I know my place as a woman!

That's when I let fly with my flamenco shoe, nailheads first. It didn't change Pio's thinking, especially since I missed. But it did shut him up.

I had thought about studying from someone else. Rosario had given me some names just before I left California: "Doloré, if Pio isn't teaching you can try—"

"What do you *mean*, 'if Pio isn't teaching!'"

There was Clotilde Morales. The social queen of Sevilla, she had cleaned up flamenco and made it respectable for the daughters of affluent Spaniards. She gave frequent concerts in big theaters with twenty-four of her adorable girls in identical costumes doing the same steps at the same time. Clotilde herself often danced in front—all three hundred pounds of her in a pink costume and a pink shawl, its pink fringe down to her fat ankles.

I couldn't see myself studying from her.

One day, I crossed the bridge to the Triana side of the river to the studio of Mario Esteban Alvarez. The class had been cancelled, no reason given. I went again the next day. The class was a rehearsal for a children's flamenco festival that evening. The third day, it was a *Sevillanas* class for little women who would tap the floor in *compás*, revolve their arms in the air, and keep up a steady stream of gossip.

I couldn't see myself there either.

The only other serious teachers were the professional flamencos who would teach for a week or two, then leave Sevilla on tour. Nothing was ever finished. There was nothing to look forward to.

In the end, I always paid what Pio asked because I didn't want to study from anyone else. I really wanted to follow the

itinerary Pio had planned for me. The dances coming: *Soleá*, *Bulerías*, and *Siguiriyas*. Especially *Siguiriyas*.

• 6 •

SIGUIRIYAS

Siguiriyas. Behind it is the whisper of Islam and the caliphate of Córdoba.

In orange groves the caliphs lounged, picked their teeth with ivory and alabaster, and watched their harems dance. From the incessant circling of the women's hips, from the rising and falling wail of the muezzins, came the winding rhythms and spiraling song of the *Siguiriyas.*

The *Siguiriyas* burns with Spain's dark side. All *cante jondo,* like the bullfights, is about love and dying.

At the end of the *Siguiriyas,* the singer, like the matador, calls to death, "We are coming, we are coming."

The bullfights invaded my life and frightened my night dreams.

In the Maestranza bullring, I saw the bull free; I saw him dead. I saw him gallop black with vivid legs into the arena, crash at the barriers, leave gouges deep as my hand. Then charge the man who approached him with silent, padding steps. Again and again, the black form dived under the matador's cape and came up white horns, lifting its massive neck with the ease of a swan, scattering the veronica cape into pink and yellow petals.

~

The matador and the bull are secret lovers in public.

The matador calls to the bull in low tones. Feet together,

ankles touching, heels off the ground, he leans into the great bulk of the animal, takes the risk that it could flick him in the air like a fly off its back. Then, his suit of lights smeared with its blood, he wraps the bull, time and again, around his own body.

As the matador courts the bull, the Gypsy woman courts the dance, invites the dangers and the discoveries.

The Gypsy woman is the mother of the bull. Her profile is the profile of the bull. She dances the *Siguiriyas* with her belly thrust forward like the bull's chest. Her breasts lift like horns. Her step is heavy, her back is bent, reclining on air. Her arms are cupped to hold the moon. She carries the bull's flanks in her buttocks. She is not slight. The weight of the caves is in her thighs; they hold up the hills.

Her *Siguiriyas* is long and slow. Swathed in her costume, she uses her skirt like the matador's cape.

I learned to dance the *Siguiriyas* from her, and from the bullfights.

Pio taught only the Gypsy *Siguiriyas*, and the Gypsy *compás*, a thorn in one's ear, unrelenting, hypnotic, not embellished. Nothing covered up the silence between the beats.

It took me weeks to learn the *compás* with its alternating accents. Every day, I cried to Pio, "I don't get it."

"*Cálmate*, Doloré. Nobody can teach *compás* like me. You'll get it."

He gave me exercises in clapping out the rhythms. He said I could practice them back at my apartment. I couldn't remember them once I left the studio.

I'd argue with him: *Siguiriyas* was impossible, I said. Nobody could count it, I said. Then Pio would count it.

"—but that still doesn't tell me where I start, Pio."

"It's easy, Doloré. You start on the seventh count of the fourth *compás* just after the singer finishes the first *copla* and just before he—"

I felt I was dancing in soup.

Some days I'd do it right. Pio would yell, "*Eso es!* Now you have it!"

But the next day, I'd do the same thing—I thought—and he'd throw his cane on the floor and bellow, "No!"

I'd cry.

There came a morning, though, when I walked into the studio and danced the *Siguiriyas* in *compás*. I couldn't understand why I ever thought it was difficult.

What came next, though, was worse than learning the *compás*: dancing the *Siguiriyas* in Pio's small studio, I'd start fast at one side and end up against a wall, running like I was on a treadmill. Pio thought it was hilarious. He'd sit and laugh and slap his knees.

I'd stop and give him a dirty look.

"*Qué te pasa, Doloré?*" he'd say. "Don't get upset. I'll show you how to do it. I can do any step in a bar or in an opera house. Look, Doloré, at this photo. Here I am dancing in Madrid for Franco—at the Opera House!"

I learned I had to solve my own problems with the *Siguiriyas*. By moving in a zig-zag pattern, I could run and yet not cover much space. And I learned to do the heelwork by focusing on a double photograph on the wall of Pio as a young man seated looking up at himself standing, both selves smiling happily at each other. His egomania piqued me and gave me the grit to keep at his heelwork until I accomplished it.

~

I loved the *Siguiriyas*. Each day that I stepped into the hot, airless, dusty studio, I danced on old Islam and Córdoba, the quiet old Spain I adored.

One morning, however, I arrived at the studio to find a roaring party in progress. Pio's family from Barcelona was there, seated in a circle laughing, jostling each other, smoking and passing around red wine and potato chips.

As soon as I entered, I knew there was a *juerga* in progress, a flamenco party. And Pio was expecting me to dance for it.

I ducked into the dressing room with Pio yelling after me, "Doloré, Doloré, you're going to dance the *Siguiriyas* for them!"

"Are you nuts?" I yelled back. "I've just learned it!"

But the Gypsies called me out. "Doloré, Doloré. *Empezemos!* Let's start!"

~

The only thing stranger than a *juerga* in the morning is dancing the *Siguiriyas* in the morning. But Pio pulled the curtain over the one window. The only light was the sun coming through the orange polka dots like little fires. With the darkness, the Gypsies became quiet, serious.

Pio, standing in a veil of smoke in the center of the studio, spoke in a sonorous voice, as if making a proclamation to the entire city of Sevilla: "My family, my aunts, my uncles, my cousins, my woman. You are all here to see my student dance the *Siguiriyas*, the *Siguiriyas* of Maestro Pio Mateo Mendoza of Sevilla, España. The best *Siguiriyas* in the whole world! *Vam' a bailar!*"

He stepped to the back of the studio and started banging out the *compás* with his cane. I came out of the dressing room and stood next to the guitarist, terrified.

The guitar played the opening chords and Joaquin, Pio's cousin, threw back his head and half-cried, half-sang the opening

"*Aiii.*" It filled the studio; it shook the window glass. It made my skin jump.

The Gypsies clapped the *compás* for me, their hands cracking like bricks. The studio was suddenly dense with sound; it bounced off the walls. I moved from the side of the guitarist to the center of the studio. The Gypsies sat so close to me I felt flayed by their presence. But my fear left; something came from them to me. A spirit rose in me. I danced on the mythic bullfight and with the authority of the Gypsy woman.

My arms reached from behind my shoulders, swept up the air in long curves. My hands circled to the *compás*, holding the music in my palms. I reached upward with my spine until I could feel space between the bones. I turned in spirals and ran, catching the bell skirt, throwing it into the air.

Ripping into the heelwork with strength, controlling the speed, I kept the tension between myself and the guitar.

My heart swinging in delighted circles, the *Siguiriyas* took my form, my face, and the Gypsies gave me back *jaleo*. *"Anda, Doloré,"* they called, *"Muchacha de España!"*

Pio took me aside after I finished and said, "You danced good, Doloré. Even if you're not Gypsy," he added.

~

After the *juerga*, there were photographs outside in the street with Pio all smiles, hamming it up in front of the cameras. Then the taxis came. Pio went with his relatives to the airport and loaded them, drunk or sober, onto the noon flight for Barcelona.

· 7 ·

CANTE JONDO

The family from Barcelona came to Sevilla in order to become porous again. To sit and sing, and listen to flamenco until it gave them back their color. They had frightened faces. They were Andalucían Gypsies who worked factory jobs and lived in cubicles with white walls. No smoky shelves with votive candles in red cups. No dancing allowed in the kitchens. They lived in high-rise concrete alongside train tracks that drained the child from their veins.

Nine of Pio's family came to stay one week, and stayed three. They slept on Pio and Aurora's floors and took their meals in shifts in Aurora's kitchen.

It wasn't long before Pio was walking around and around the studio, haggard and penniless, holding his head with both hands and saying, "My God! How they eat!"

But Aurora was happy when she was caring for the family, tucking in the corners of their lives.

Early in the mornings, she would step around the people asleep on her floors and go shopping for fresh fried *churros*. At breakfast, the family sat at the card table in the kitchen holding mugs of black coffee and eating the *churros* straight out of the white wrapping paper.

After breakfast, she coaxed what money she could out of Pio and went shopping at the open air market.

The rest of the day, the women sat together at the kitchen

41

table preparing food, while Aurora cooked. They sang quick, happy snatches of the *Bulerías*. Aurora stood at her big stove, waving her spatula in one hand and swinging her big hips to the *compás*.

But by night, the same women sat around the same card table and sang the *Siguiriyas* low so the men watching TV in the living room couldn't hear them. They sang their hatred for their lives in Barcelona:

"*Aiii...* We live in boxes and never see the hills."
"But you have money," Aurora would reply.
"*Aiii...* What's money? You can't talk to it or hold it in your
     lap."
"But you have each other."
"*Aiii...* We are alone. And unknown."
"But there are other Gypsies there."
"*Aiii...* They are different from us."
"Different?"
"*Aiii...* They do not sing."
"How can they live?" replied Aurora.

~

Pio had returned elated from the airport; his relatives were gone. But Aurora cried; she wanted to be with her family in Alcalá, a small white village fifty miles outside Sevilla where most of Pio and Aurora's clan lived.

Pio protested but they took the bus to Alcalá. Pio, who couldn't drive, sat in the front seat next to the driver, waving his arms like a windmill and shouting directions at him. Meanwhile Aurora sat in the back seat saying, "Are we lost yet? Are we lost yet?"

When they got to Alcalá, they walked from the bus stop to

Pio's family home where his father lived.

Pio's father was called *Teo el Cojo*. He was small, like a mouse. He had the same fear in his eyes. He had no teeth, and one leg not there from the knee down. Although he was the oldest man in the clan, he never had any say in how it was run.

When his wife Margarita died, old Teo went to his bed in his nightshirt and stayed there for nine years. He decided he was dying. At first the family took him to doctors, who said there was nothing wrong with him and gave him white pills in white envelopes. But the old man still wouldn't get out of bed. His daughters, Macarena, Benita, and Constancia, took care of him.

After two years in bed, the family agreed with him—he was dying. They stopped taking him to doctors.

After five years, old Teo began having visions. He'd see a reflection of light on the wall in the shape of a cross and call his daughters and grandchildren. With everyone around him, he'd clasp his rosary to his chest, say he was glad to be going and announce he would be dead by morning. The family would say, "Yes, father. We will have a *juerga* for you to celebrate your passing to Glory." They had many all-night *juergas* with everyone singing and dancing. The old man enjoyed them all.

But the morning he woke up twitching all over and gasping for air, he said he did not want to die. He wanted to go to the hospital.

That was the morning Aurora and Pio arrived.

~

I heard the whole story from Aurora when they got back after only two days in Alcalá.

Aurora had invited me to lunch, but when I got to their apartment she wasn't in the kitchen cooking. She was sitting on the living room couch, the foam rubber coming through the naugahyde. I sat down across from her in their rickety rocking chair. She was sniffling and picking at a tissue. I had wondered why they had returned early from Alcalá but had been shy about asking. But when Aurora started to cry, I asked, "I know you returned early from Alcalá. Why, Aurora?"

"Doloré," she said between sniffles, "as soon as we got to Alcalá, there was my cousin Jerónimo carrying old Teo down the middle of the street. And everyone was running behind him and yelling, 'He's dying! He's dying!' I tried to run, but I couldn't and they all left me behind. Then they got Teo into a taxi and they went to the hospital. Pio, too."

Aurora took another tissue out of her apron pocket, dabbed at her eyes and went on, "So I sat on the curb to wait."

"How long did you have to wait?"

"Oh, they came back fast. Jerónimo and Nemesio, they were walking old Teo down the street, holding him up. They said, 'He's not dying. He's not dying. The doctors said so.' But Teo kept saying, 'What do those dumb doctors know?' Well, they finally got him up the steps and into his house and Macarena and Benita put him to bed and Constancia started to make him some soup. Pio just sat there and said, `I told you. I told you he wasn't dying.'

"But I went in the back room by myself. I was burning up inside."

"You were thinking the doctors were wrong?"

"Sí, Doloré. I thought maybe Teo really was dying. The doctors, they were wrong when they cut open my throat. They said I had something bad, but when they cut it open they said it wasn't bad. But then they took out the thing I sang with just to be sure. I thought maybe they were wrong again.

"So I put out the cards on a table. Then I lit three candles and right in front of me was the Death card. I knew. And I ran into the front room and said as loud as I could, 'He is dying! He is!'"

"That must have scared everybody."

"Oh, *sí*. Macarena and Benita, they started to cry. And Constancia, she was trying to put the soup down the old man, and she spilled it all over him. Pio yelled at me, 'Aurora, you old fart! What'd you go and say that for?'"

"So what did you say back to Pio?"

"Doloré, I told him about the cards. Pio, he didn't listen to me. But old Teo, he just sat straight up in bed and said, 'See. See. I told you. I'm going.' And Pio said, 'Old man, you're not going anywhere.'"

"Teo, he laid back down and he said straight to Pio, 'My oldest son is dead, and I'm stuck with the likes of you to carry on my name.' Pio, he got so mad, I was scared he was going to hit the old man. And he yelled at him, 'What did I ever do to you, old man, but make money so you can lie in bed all day and moan about a woman you were never fit to touch!' Then Teo yelled back, 'Don't you talk to me about touching women. You *sinvergüenza*. You *libertino*. You touch the wrong ones!'"

"Constancia, she was trying to calm everybody down and clean up the soup on the old man. She said, 'Father, Teodoro is long dead. Pio is your oldest son now. Like it or not.' And the old man pushed Constancia away and said, 'I don't like it!' and spilled more soup on himself. Well, Pio's face just went white, except for his scar. It got bright red. And I said to myself, 'This is an omen.'"

"You mean you knew what was going to happen next?"

"*Sí*, Doloré. And I was right. Old Teo, he began shaking and he could hardly breathe. And he said, 'Women. Make me a *juerga* so I can die with my friends and family around me.'"

"What did Pio do?" I asked.

"Oh, Pio, he just left the house and slammed the door. But Macarena, she went out and ran up and down the street and told everybody and pretty soon people came. Even Pio, 'cause the bar was closed. And the men put Teo's big iron bed in the middle of the room and chairs around it and everybody sat and drank wine and talked. And Nemesio started playing his guitar. Old Rafael, he sang *Bulerías* first. He sings like he has rags in his mouth but he has the *gusto*. I thought maybe Pio would dance for Teo. But he wouldn't. Old Antonito, though, he did, right beside Teo's bed. And Teo said to him, 'Thank you, my friend, for dancing me to Glory.'

"Then Joaquin started singing. He sang low and cried in his song for the time he lost his woman because she wasn't *Calé* so he had to leave her. He broke off the song, but Macarena picked it up and sang about when her husband left her for another woman.

"Well, after that, Tía Sofía started the *Siguiriyas*. And I knew if the old man was going to die, it would be soon. 'Cause she sang about the war, Doloré."

"The big guns, they were right outside of Alcalá?"

"*Sí.* And she sang how we were all living in caves then and the morning the cave fell in, it fell on little Alicia and little Teodoro while they were eating. It was hours before we got them out. And when we did, they were dead.

"So we laid them on the ground outside the cave. I was little, and I had never seen anyone dead before. They looked gray and they had food in their mouths and mud on their faces. I was shivering 'cause it was raining. I thought maybe they were shivering too; I wanted to make them warm."

I took Aurora's hand but said nothing. I had never seen war

close up. I couldn't begin to speak to her pain.

Aurora and I sat without talking for a moment, then she went on, "We all sat around them on the wet ground. Nobody could sing at first. But then my father, he started singing *Soleá*. He sang so loud and so high I thought my ears would break. And when he stopped, somebody else sang. And we sat there in the rain and sang all the rest of the day and all that night 'til the sun came up. Then we all went down to the cemetery and buried the children."

Aurora looked down at her hands as she spoke, "When Tía Sofía finished the song, old Teo, he closed his eyes. And I thought, 'This is it,' and crossed myself. Everybody else thought the same thing and we were all silent. But he only started snoring.

"So we all sat for a while and talked. Then we started leaving, one person here, one person there. All except Constancia. She stayed the whole night with old Teo. Me and Pio, we walked on down to the *pensión*. Pio kept saying, 'See. I told you! I told you he wasn't dying!'

"And Pio was right. The next day Teo, he got up out of bed and sat outside and Constancia took his picture. Pio was so mad at his father we came right back to Sevilla."

Teary, Aurora sniffled once and said, "And, Doloré, I didn't get to be with my family."

∙ 8 ∙

AURORA
Born ?, Died November 27, 1990

She was not born. But she died.

The date of her dying is written in a book in the City Hall of Sevilla specifying the nature of her illness, the time of her death, the hospital, the doctor present.

But her birth was never recorded. She was a Gypsy.

~

Aurora, the youngest of twelve children, nine of whom were delivered by a midwife who was blind in one eye, a live snake in her apron pocket, was born in a cave, thick with the smell of smoking olive oil. In a back 'room' her mother lay spread-legged on a dirty mattress. Other women sat around her. It was a difficult delivery. The women broke pieces of string so the baby would be born free of the umbilical cord. They sang low to keep The Evil One away. But Aurora's mother died as her baby was being born. Aurora was wrapped in an old blanket and handed to her grandmother, Sofía, to raise.

~

Out of war and poverty, Aurora grew up ragged, dirty, and skinny. She played with gutter sticks for dolls.

Meanwhile, Pio was knife-fighting in the streets over banana peels thrown away by tourists.

Aurora and Pio were betrothed in infancy. It was considered

49

a good match: they were close in ages, members of the same clan, and first cousins.

Aurora and Pio watched each other grow up in the street dust of Alcalá. He saw her dark skinned, thin between the shoulder blades, at nine already half a head taller than he was.

She saw Pio as a fast-running little bull, fists on feet, able to knock out full-grown men and bring blood to their eyes.

At ten, Aurora's bosoms began to bloom. Pio wanted to touch them, though he knew he mustn't.

And when she saw the breezes blowing his long black curls, little wiggles of aching went through her. She cried when he put his hands on another girl's bottom.

At eleven, Aurora's nose spread out over her face; Pio moaned inside his soul. But he liked to listen to her singing. Her voice, an arrow to open the sky, made him feel a sweetness towards her.

About that same time, Pio was teaching himself to dance. He asked help from other dancers. They showed him their steps and he did them—only better. Aurora would watch and then run bragging about him to her girl friends.

When she began menstruating at twelve, Sofía and the other women whispered at the street corners as they crocheted. They said Pio's name, then hers. "She's still a child. Give her time," they said, "two years, maybe three, before she marries."

Aurora was fifteen and Pio sixteen when they married.

~

They had a modest wedding. Two hundred Gypsies moved into Alcalá for three days and nights of festivities.

The Gypsies came in battered cars loaded with chairs, tables, bedding, pots, pans, live chickens, and children, their heads sticking out of the windows along with the sausages and loaves of bread.

The Gypsies built fires in the municipal park, put up tents for the children, set tables end-to-end down the main street of Alcalá. No one in Alcalá slept for three days—not the Gypsies, not the Spaniards, and not the Guardias.

The night before the wedding, the *Sevillanas* was danced in the street. Pio and Aurora started dancing on opposite sides of the street and changed partners until they came to each other. In the *pasado,* Pio touched Aurora for the first time. Electricity twanged through her body; Pio was trembling. They went on dancing, touching each other only with their fingertips. Nobody noticed when they left together—nobody but Sofía, Aurora and Pio's common grandmother, who had killed a chicken that afternoon.

That night, on an old mattress in the back of Sofía's cave, Pio and Aurora were married. The morning of their wedding, it was Sofía who tested Aurora's honor. The white handkerchief, flown like a banner at the head table, was spotted bright with blood, one or two chicken feathers still sticking to it.

~

Pio, performing in Paris, took Aurora there for their honeymoon, the first and last time she left Spain. Back in Sevilla, expecting a large family, he rented a flat with four bedrooms in a fine new building near the Alameda de Hercules.

Every night, Aurora would grab the big kiss of love and rock her hips under Pio's; every night she would wish for a baby.

But no babies came and Pio started staying away more and more.

Aurora sat alone in her empty flat imagining miracles and weaving Pio into the songs she sang:

"*Aiii...* Pio, he is on a white horse. He rides across

the Roman bridge and up the boulevard to the big store. Everybody on the street follows him in. They watch him buy a white *cordebés* and they beg him, 'Write our names on the band in dark letters.'

"*Aiii...* Then no one is there. It is very quiet. All the merchandise is still. Nothing is moving. Pio feels tears on his cheeks. But they are not his. They belong to someone else. 'Where do you come from,' he says to the tears.

"*Aiii...* They answer, 'We are hers, Aurora's. She has a big flat with lots of bedrooms. But she has no children.'"

~

Aurora knew the magical arts of her tribe: she buried an egg wrapped in a cloth soaked with Pio's urine in the bank of the river and sat next to it under a full moon. She collected rain water and passed it through a sieve. She burned special herbs, breathing in their smoke. She never took off the talisman Sofía had given her.

But no babies came, and Aurora was without the one thing to make her marriage real. The women of her clan pitied her. She avoided their eyes, never asking them about their children.

Pio, who had given Aurora his undivided attention for a year, began spending his time with the young women around him—the ambitious young dancers, the attractive *aficionadas* at the stage door.

~

It was Joselito who told me about Pio's women. "You know, Doloré," he would say, "Pio, he lit up the stage like a light bulb. Audiences loved him. But backstage, the women ran for their lives. In those tight skirts, he couldn't keep his hands off them. And the madder they got, the more he liked it. He was a *libertino. Me entiende,* Doloré?"

"Oh, I understand. We have a word for it in English—'lech.'"

"And after a while, Doloré, Pio wanted all women, everywhere. You know, the train would pull into a city, maybe Paris or Madrid, and he'd get all dressed up in a white suit and a white *cordobés* at just the right angle over his eyebrows. He'd have two tall blondes, one on each arm. And he'd walk up and down the main street so everybody would see him."

"Meanwhile," I said, "Aurora sat at home and she didn't know."

"Oh, she knew in her heart, Doloré." Joselito sighed, "She is dumb, Doloré, but she's not *that* dumb. He couldn't keep it from Aurora. The first few women were a shock to her. But after a while, she gave up counting. But not complaining. She'd tell her troubles to Sofía. She'd call Sofía and tell her that at night in bed, she could smell another woman on Pio, that he was cheating on her again.

"'So? Let him cheat,' Sofía would say back to her, 'At least you know where he is.'

"But in truth, Doloré, Aurora seldom knew where Pio was."

~

I only knew the young Aurora from the photographs in Pio's studio: Aurora the bride, tall, slender, smiling. Years later, singing at a party, she had a big bosom and a bigger belly, but there was a waist in between.

By the time I met Aurora, her body had collapsed into corpulence. Her jowls sunk into her thick neck; her heavy breasts hung on her belly, a sea of flesh. There were times she could not sleep lying down for fear of suffocating.

She had lost all of her singing voice, and much of her speaking voice, to a needless operation. When Aurora was little, she had been told she would follow in her father Esteban's footsteps. He was the best of the *cante jondo* singers in Spain. He excelled in the *Siguiriyas*, the deepest of the deep songs. Even in the tawdriest bars on the worst nights, people would be silent to hear him.

Aurora could sing like her father. But she could also sing the *cante chico*, the joyous songs of flamenco: *Alegrías, Bulerías, Fandangos, Caracoles*. When she was young, she sang like no woman since Pastora Pavón.

The first time I met her, however, I thought her an imbecile. She spoke in hoarse grunts and raspy whispers. But after many visits to their flat, sitting with her under the peeling wallpaper, eating or watching television, I could understand her.

I loved to listen to this gentle, concerned woman who watched over everyone in the clan, who held together the insides of Pio, and who eventually raised as her own four of his children by other women.

Undone by the loss of her singing voice, Aurora made up for it by talking, despite her difficulty speaking.

Once, I asked Aurora how long she had been married to Pio.

"Forty-three years," she said, "but he's made me cry a lot."

"And that's okay with you?"

"Well," she said, "I'd say to him, 'Pio, you're making me cry a lot.' And he'd say, 'It doesn't matter. I love you. I don't love them.' And I'd say, 'Well, if you don't love them, why do you sleep with them?' And he'd say, 'Aurora, you're no prize.' And I'd say, 'And you are?' And he'd say, 'I'm the best dancer in all of Spain!' And I'd say, 'You're still a head shorter than me even if you have an elephant's prick.' And he'd laugh and I'd laugh and we'd hold hands. Because we were kids together and we love each other. I don't know what else to tell you."

• 9 •

EL CORONIL

Pio on his morning picture walks omitted photographs that weren't of himself. But one day I put a finger on a small photograph of a young woman in the traditional riding costume: black trousers, cropped jacket, ruffled white shirt, a black *cordobés* across her head. "And who is this?" I asked.

Pio was delighted I was taking an interest in his photos. "Graciela," he replied, "of El Coronil. She bore me two sons."

And in the very next breath, "But look here, Doloré. Here I am in Barcelona!"

~

One Friday, after my lesson, Pio told me he and Joselito were going to El Coronil for a *festival* of flamenco *cante*. Pio had taught my lesson dressed up in a white suit, not too clean, a black shirt with big white polka dots, and a red scarf around his skinny neck. Joselito looked no different than he ever did.

I walked with them as far as the bus station. Joselito said it would be a short walk. The streets were short; the walk was long.

Joselito never stopped talking about the *barrio*, its Gypsies, its artists, its saints.

But I was listening to Pio's silence: the last ship out of an Hieronymus Bosch painting, an upside down man floating naked over a lake, luminous orange eggs in a faded blue sky. This was Pio's mind.

There was also another image in Pio's mind: a slight, small-waisted woman with a mass of light brown hair, steel blue eyes, and a chiseled profile. She had the look of a silk-embroidered bloodline, and the smell of money on chiffon. Graciela.

~

Pio danced one night at a flamenco *festival* held in the big corral of a bull ranch outside of El Coronil.

The boy who burned the stage in streaks had become the man who danced beyond dazzle. Pio, never subtle in his talk, became subtle in his dance. What the audience saw was a bird darting, perplexing the sky, changing its direction as quickly as light. His heelwork, a tightly woven texture, was the chatter of insects at night. The audience held its breath to hear it.

He performed alone for five hundred people. In the front row center was the owner of the ranch, Graciela. She followed the rolling swing of his pelvis with her eyes.

~

Afterwards, she introduced herself to Pio, reached out, took his hand in hers and invited him to dinner—in her patio.

It was Joselito, of course, who knew the Graciela story. Seated across from one another in one of the bars, he told it to me.

"Doloré, that night in her patio by candlelight, Graciela talked. She told Pio of her travels, her education, the titles in her family, all the important people she knew. Pio, he knew only his name. So he shut up and listened. Graciela, she talked about every bull on the ranch, and how wide their horns were. What their names were. And how she loved to ride out with the men for the *rejoneo* and tilt the young bulls over on their backs. Then she asked Pio to talk about himself."

"That was a mistake," I muttered.

"*Sí*, no one ever asks Pio to talk about himself. But she wanted to know about his children. Well, Aurora and Pio had been married fifteen years and were childless when Pio met Graciela. So, Pio, he coughed in his soup, and blew bubbles in his mouth to cover up his words, 'I have no children.' But Graciela heard him and she said, 'Neither have I.'"

"Quite a coincidence," I said.

"*Sí*, Doloré. Then Pio asked her, 'Forgive, but where is your *marido*?' And Graciela said, 'I have no *marido*. I left my husband because he didn't give me babies. No man has ever been able to give me babies.'

"Pio, he stopped eating with his fork halfway to his mouth and said straight out to her, 'I can get you pregnant.' And then he took another bite of food.

"Graciela, she looked across the table at him and said, 'Maybe you can—maybe you can.'

"Pio started to explain, 'You see, it's my wife. She can't—'

"But Graciela interrupted him, 'I don't want to hear. You may come to my bed tonight. And if I get pregnant, we will be lovers. But if I don't get pregnant tonight, I never want to see you again.'

"Then, Graciela, she asked him, 'Are you pure-blooded?' '*Si!*' Pio said, '*Gitano puro!*' And she said, 'Good. Then our children will sing.'"

Joselito stopped talking, as if he was getting up to leave.

"Oh, Joselito," I pleaded, "it's a wonderful story. Don't stop now."

Joselito sat back down and lit another cigarette, "Well," he went on, "the next morning, Pio and Graciela went out to the big corral to watch the young bulls being branded. Then Pio went back to Sevilla. A month or so later, he was coming off the stage and into his dressing room. And there was Graciela, sitting at his make-up table, a big smile on her face. She took his hand in hers and said, 'Tonight we will drive back to El Coronil.'

"Well, their first son was Carlos Antonio Enrique, named after Graciela's father, grandfather, and great grandfather. And two years later came Jorge, their second son. Graciela named him after her great, great grandfather.

"Graciela, she moved like a dot of light in Pio's life. She was seen everywhere with him. He told everybody—but Aurora—about his two sons. 'They have black curly hair, like mine,' he'd say, 'And they're small, like me.' Graciela and Pio, for five years, they were a couple."

"And Aurora," I asked, "she never found out about Graciela?"

"Oh, not yet, Doloré," Joselito went on, "not 'til the end. Graciela, you know, she liked to tilt the bulls. But this one bull, his name was El Rey, well, he tilted her instead—broke her neck."

"Oh, my God!"

"It was bad. *Sí*. When she was dying, Pio, he went to her. He sat by her bed and held her hand. He told her how much he wanted the boys. How much Aurora always wanted children. But Graciela wouldn't have it. She told him her family would raise the boys. Of course, they would never be told they were half Gypsy. Then the doctor walked Pio to the front door. Pio, he asked him, 'When does she die?' And the doctor replied, 'Soon.'"

"And did she die?"

"Oh, *sí*. And when she died, then Aurora found out 'cause Graciela's picture was in the newspaper, along with Pio's and the two little boys. Well, Aurora, she can't read or write, Doloré. But she understood the resemblance between Pio and the boys.

"She sat all day in that old sunken sofa of hers with the newspaper photo in her hands. Pio, he came home that night, and Aurora showed it to him. He didn't deny it. He just said, 'Aurora, you understand, I never loved Graciela.'

"But Aurora didn't understand. She told Pio she wished he had died right along with Graciela. She would have buried him beside her!

"Well, Pio, he got mad and he yelled, 'You're not my woman anymore!' And he went into the kitchen and slammed the door. Aurora, she sat for a long time on the sofa. Then she got up and took the night bus to Alcalá and went home to Sofía and told her the whole story. And Sofía said, 'So, Aurora. What is it you want?'

" 'I want Pio,' she said.

" '*Mare de Dios!* Why?'

" 'He can't live without me.'

" 'True,' Sofía said, 'but let him find that out for himself.'

"Pio, he found out all right, Doloré. Without Aurora, he shatters like an eggshell. He walked around their flat for a full week looking for her, calling her name. He looked for her in the closets and behind the furniture. He even opened drawers. He couldn't sleep. He couldn't eat. He missed his own performances. Finally, after a week of this, he sat down and stared at the telephone for a whole day. Then he called Alcalá. But Pio, he never said he was sorry to Aurora. He didn't apologize. Nothing like that. No. He just said, 'Aurora, without you, I can't dance.'"

"And Aurora came back."

"*Sí*, Doloré. She came back."

~

Monday morning I arrived for my lesson. Pio was late;

Joselito was on time. We waited on the sidewalk. Joselito smoked as he talked, "Doloré, when we got to El Coronil, we missed the bus out to the *festival*. So, we had to walk—four miles!"

"Oh, Joselito. In the heat?"

"*Sí*, Doloré. *Increíble!* Pio, he waved and smiled at every car that passed. But nobody stopped. After a while he gave up the waving and smiling. He started yelling at the cars, 'You *sinvergüenzas!* You stupid people! You should recognize me!'

"But we kept walking. We had walked maybe two miles. Then Pio, he saw this big house across a field of sunflowers, all black and dead. And Pio, without a word to me, starts running across the field, black dust all over his white trousers. I yelled, 'Where the hell do you think you're going?' But he didn't answer. So what could I do? I followed him. The house, Doloré, it was empty. And a mess, the roof caved in. Even so, I could tell it had been a big ranch. Pio, he went right through the house and out to the patio, full of weeds and broken tiles, and out to a big corral. He knew his way around. Then he just stood there in the center of the corral. So I asked him, 'What are we here for?' Pio, he didn't answer for a moment. Then he said, 'I danced here, for five hundred people."

"Was this her house—Graciela's?'"

"I already guessed that, Doloré. And then, Pio, he said, 'She bore me two sons.' I knew that too. Then he picked up a handful of dirt and let it fall through his fingers and said, 'I don't know where they are. What's happened to them. I haven't seen them since they were little.' That was all he said. So we left.

"But oh, at the *festival,* once we got there, Pio spent the whole time talking. Up and down the table, up and down—telling everybody who he was. Where he had danced. And all about Graciela and their two sons. He talked so much people were yelling at him to shut up.

"I tell you, Doloré, I will never go to another *festival* with Pio."

~

When Pio arrived and opened the studio, Joselito entered without a word, not even saying his *muy buenos*, while Pio said nothing about the *festival* at El Coronil. So I asked him, "Well—how was it?"

"Nothing exceptional," he replied.

"Really?" I said, "I heard there were some good singers."

"Oh, *sí*. But the audience! Once they knew who I was, Doloré, I had to tell them everything. Where I danced. When. Everything. They talked so much I couldn't hear the singing. Stupid people."

· 10 ·

CASA CHICA

"Doloré." Aurora once asked me, "Do *payos* dream? 'Cause I thought maybe only Gypsies dream."

"No," I answered, "we dream too."

"Doloré, I dream a lot about Pio. 'Cause he's never here. So I dream about him. That way he is here. And he tells me things in my dreams that he never told me.

"Like the dream where Pio saw a shadow on a wall. It was hers, Graciela's. When he put his hand on the shadow, it moved. It ran across the wall and it ran out to a big corral, and Pio, he ran after it. And in the middle of the corral, there was this grave. It was hers. But it was only her shadow buried there.

"I woke up crying, Doloré, 'cause even after she was dead it was like she was still here. I couldn't stop thinking about her and Pio. And the two little boys. I wanted children so bad and Pio couldn't make them with me."

Which didn't explain Pio and Aurora's four children.

~

I met all their children—Diego, Teresita, and the twins, Manolo and Raul—when I still thought they were Pio and Aurora's children.

Teresita I met first, but she didn't meet me.

Teresita sat, all day, every day, in the half-light of her little room in the back of the flat. She never wanted to leave it. She sat with her fingers in her mouth, babbling and laughing to herself. Teresita was twenty-seven years old when I 'met' her. There was no acknowledgement in her eyes as Aurora went through the small formality of placing her hand in mine, and shaking her hand for her.

"Teresita," Aurora had told me, "she got born all wrong, Doloré. Everybody knew from the beginning she wasn't right. But I begged to have her. 'Cause she was our cousin Marta's baby. Pio, he wouldn't say it was his baby but Marta told me it was.

"People say that we're bad 'cause we have babies together in the clan. But, Doloré, it's all family. Anyway, Marta, she was only fifteen. And she was scared of Teresita 'cause she was all wrong. But me, I didn't mind. I wanted Teresita. Teresita is as close as I'll ever get to having Pio's baby."

~

Teresita was not unusual; Pio's clan preferred first cousin marriages. Never mind the consequences. Like Angel, the little four-year-old athlete with smart eyes and a bright face. But his left hand, perfect slender fingers and pink pearl nails, was a small bird's wing growing out of his left shoulder.

~

Diego I met next. I liked Diego. But I rarely saw him. He worked double-shifts as a bartender. He was saving his money to open his own bar. Diego was calm, self-assured, rational. God, I thought, how did he ever come out of that bunch!

Over time, I learned *how*.

It was in Pio's last 'Graciela' year that Diego was born to the prostitute, Maria.

The night she ran terrified and screaming from the brothel, Pio picked her up in his taxi and took her to his flat. He gave her red wine in the kitchen and Aurora bathed her head with cool water.

They let her sleep in the back bedroom. She stayed on and cleaned house for Aurora.

Pio visited her late one night. Maria swore Diego was his child. Pio swore her belly was already round.

When Diego was born, Maria asked Aurora to take him so she could go back to work.

Pio said, "He's the son of a *puta!*"

Aurora said, "A child's a child. Who cares where it comes from?"

And since that was the year Aurora got anything she wanted, she took Diego and loved him as her own.

~

Then I met Manolo. He came up to my apartment. Aurora had sent him to invite me to dinner. He had tried at the studio; I wasn't there. So he asked around the *barrio* where "the American woman who dances and she's not young" lived. He said it took less than five minutes to get my address.

I had just washed my floors and he tracked in dirt. When he saw it, he apologized and offered to wash my floor again. I said no, and we sat and had white wine and talked. He was eighteen and waiting to be called into the *mili,* the military, just hanging out on the streets, dealing a little, doing nothing—waiting. He was pleasant; I was confused. He was tall, lanky, skinny. I didn't see how he could be Pio and Aurora's son.

I learned yet another *how.*

Pio had loved Graciela like a sailor loves a ship he cannot sail. But even before she died, he had gone back to tall blondes.

He was under contract to dance twice a year in the tourist night club in Málaga. But Pio didn't like Málaga; he never liked beaches.

His solution was to start his *casa chica* in Málaga. He found a house to rent all year round—one away from the beach. Then he looked for a woman. He wanted a tall blonde. There weren't any; the *malagueñas* are short and dark.

Except Paula. A fisherman's daughter, young, pretty, poor. But for a *malagueña*, exceptionally tall, and willing to bleach her hair for Pio.

At eighteen, she wanted nothing so much in this world as to be a dancer. Pio made her lots of promises and she moved into the little house.

But Pio's *casa chica* blew up in his face when Paula got pregnant. The baby came, but Pio denied it was his, saying he wasn't even in Málaga "at the time." The more he said it wasn't his, the more Paula said it was. Pio got annoyed and went to Málaga to close up the house, not counting on Paula's father, a burly man twice Pio's size.

While Pio was inside the house, Paula's father was outside, banging on the front door with both hands and yelling, "Open this goddamn door or I'll kill you!"

Pio, like a frightened bird, flew around the walls of the house until he found a back window out.

Aurora told me that a few days later, as she was coming up the stairs of the flat, a string bag of groceries in each hand, she saw Paula's father standing in front of the door to the flat.

"Doloré," Aurora said, "there he was, that big man, and he yells, 'Is this where Pio Mendoza lives? That miserable *hijo de puta!* I'm gonna kill the bastard! He got my Paula pregnant.'

"Well, Doloré, I couldn't say anything. I was so scared, I dropped all my groceries and started to cry.

"And he looked at me and he said, 'Who are you? Are you

his woman?'

"Well, I still couldn't talk. I just opened the door and went into the kitchen and sat down and cried some more. And the man, he followed me in. I was so afraid he was going to hit me. He just stood with his back to the sink and looked real mad. But then he said he was sorry he scared me.

"And he said, 'My Paula, she's a pretty girl. She has a chance now at a good marriage. I want this marriage for her. It can't happen now, you understand, *señora*. 'Cause she's got this bastard baby. No offense intended, *señora*, but by a Gypsy! And I've come to tell your husband he has to take the baby. If he won't, I'll wring his neck! *Por Dios,* I will do it!'

"His voice was so loud, Doloré, my heart started beating real hard. But, I said to him, and I made the words the best I could, I said, 'Your Paula, she would give up the baby?'

" 'She'll give it up 'cause I say so!'

"Then he says to me, 'You are Pio's woman? You would take the baby?'

" 'Oh!' I said, '*Sí!*' I couldn't believe I was so lucky, Doloré. Then he says the baby is a boy and his name is Manolo. Then he left.

"When Pio got home, I told him everything. Except I lied. 'Cause I told Pio the man had a gun.

"Well, Pio, he was so scared he said yes. But he still says Manolo isn't his baby and Paula was a little *puta* and sleeping all over Málaga."

~

Raul. I met him last. Short and pudgy, bursting the seams of his uniform, he was in the *mili*, on leave, and staying with Pio and Aurora. One day as I came in the flat, he was arguing with Pio over money. In the middle of a barrage of obscenities coming from Pio, Aurora introduced me to Raul as Manolo's 'twin'.

It seemed that soon after Manolo was put into Aurora's arms, Maria had come back to the flat with a newborn baby boy—Raul.

Aurora wanted to take him. But Pio yelled, "What are we running here! An orphanage for *putas*?"

"But she said it was your baby, Pio."

"You believe everything you hear?"

"But, Pio, anyway, what's one more baby?"

"One more? That makes four and God knows who shows up at the door next!"

Aurora thought it over and called the Casa Tito Bar in Alcalá to talk to Sofía. Sofía came lumbering down to the bar on her whale legs. Aurora asked her if she should take the baby. "It's Pio's by another woman," she said.

"So, Aurora, what's different about that?"

"Pio says it's not his. Maria says it is."

"I believe her before Pio."

"But Sofía, she's a *puta*."

"So what does that make Pio?"

After the call, Aurora told Pio, "Sofía says I should take the baby."

"Her you believe. *Me* you don't! Anyway, I told you I don't want another baby. And it's not mine. You think I'd go into a dump like that?"

"It's not a dump, Pio. They have TV."

"You go inside?"

"*Sí.* Maria and me are friends."

"I don't want you being friends with a *puta!*"

"They're not bad, Pio, just poor. Like Gypsies."

"They're not like Gypsies. Gypsy women don't do that."

"Oh, *sí*, Pio. There was that Gypsy. Her name was—"

"Aurora, shut up!"

But Aurora didn't shut up. "Doloré," she said, "I told Pio I wanted two little boys like twins. Like the babies he had by that woman. They were like twins. She dressed them alike and they looked alike. And I told Pio if he wouldn't let me take Raul, I would leave with Diego and Teresita and Manolo and I would never come back.

"Well Pio, he didn't say yes or no. He just went back to Madrid to dance. So I took Raul."

~

As Manolo and Raul grew up, Aurora would walk in the sun, one 'twin' in each hand. She dressed them in small sailor suits and blue caps with "La Armada de España" embroidered in bright red thread.

"They're just like the little boys Pio had by Graciela," Aurora would say, "just like them."

· 11 ·

ALCALÁ

One afternoon, late August, Manolo came up to my apartment—he knew where it was this time—to tell me Rosario was arriving from California soon. I asked specifically *when*? Manolo said it again, *soon.* Gypsy time.

Two nights later, Manolo came up the five flights to say, "He's here." Nothing more.

I was elated. But I waited until morning to go over to the flat.

It was Sunday. Sevilla on Sundays is an unconcerned old city. The air slipping through the narrow alleyways carries history. I could feel the ancient Islamic world mixed with the present. I enjoyed the empty streets, the calm, the quiet—which was good because when I got to the flat, Rosario and Pio were yelling at each other in the living room while Aurora was crying in the kitchen.

I had hardly said hello to Rosario before he told me, voice shaking, that he wanted to stay at his father's house. Would I drive him—right now—to Alcalá?

So I did. In a borrowed car, little more than an umbrella on wheels. With uncertain forward gears and a reverse gear that wasn't working at all, we advanced through the landscape of Andalucía, spotted as a beetle's back with olive trees. I took backroads that cut through old groves, the trees thick, fat, and gnarled, their leaves, silver mirrors to the sun, the black pits left to flesh out or fall fallow to the ground. I drove through towns, white and quiet as reclining

71

ghosts, two or three men playing dominoes at card tables in the street, women in black standing, watching for the next move.

~

This was not my first trip to Alcalá.

In California, Rosario had said to me, "Doloré, I want you to meet my family in Alcalá. See the house we lived in, all of us together. And I want you to take my father a barbecue. 'Cause there's a patio. It's small. So I'll buy him a small barbecue. Will you Doloré? Will you take the barbecue to Alcalá?"

I said yes to the barbecue, wondering how I was going to pack it. The closer it came time to leave, the less I heard of it— gladly. In the end, the barbecue became a check for thirty dollars from Rosario to his father and a calendar with a picture of the Golden Gate Bridge at sunset.

Rosario had told me how to get to Alcalá: "Doloré," he said, "you go to the Bar Naranjito in Sevilla. Have a drink and hang around. You don't ask about the special taxi to Alcalá. No. 'Cause you'll get stuck with the whole fare. You wait until someone asks the bartender about the taxi. Then you say,'I'm going there too!' Then, when you get to Alcalá, you ask anyone for the Pensión Nemesio. And you get a room right away 'cause it's the only *pensión* in Alcalá. Then you ask Nemesio where the Casa Tito bar is. And when you get there, you have a drink and ask anyone where old Teo lives. Someone will be glad to take you up the hill."

But Rosario's plan fell apart right from the beginning because there were three bars 'Naranjito' in Sevilla, and none of them knew anything about a special taxi to Alcalá. I took a bus.

Once in Alcalá, I found the *pensión* and Nemesio. I was telling him about coming from California with gifts from Rosario when an elderly man with a cane passed us in the hallway. I didn't think he overheard our conversation, but minutes later when I went out on the street, I was met by the same man and half a dozen other people I didn't know. But they knew who I was, where I was from, and what I was doing in Alcalá. They bought me a glass of red wine in the Bar Tito.

The Bar Tito was two stories. Downstairs—plain, a bar, a few stools, a few tables and chairs. Upstairs—even plainer, a room with chairs in a semi-circle, a low table for drinks. Tito provided the space. The flamencos of Alcalá filled it.

After a reasonable amount of time talking and drinking, I was escorted to the front door of Teo's house. I walked in as if expected. Rosario had told me in California that he was sending letters ahead to the family in Alcalá.

It was noon. Rosario's old father was sitting in his nightshirt in a wooden chair. Benita was opposite him, her kneecaps touching his, feeding him grapes like a baby bird, one by one.

I handed Teo the check and the calendar. There was a neediness in the way he grasped the check.

~

I had learned the hard early history of the clan, not from Rosario, who seemed to know little, but from Pio, who knew it all.

A stolen guitar? Pio would know where it was, who had it. A dark evil, buried with the perpetrator? Pio could tell the whole story. Pio would want money, however; even memory was a marketable commodity.

No one, including myself, asked him anything. Sometimes, though, he would let things slip. On his picture walk one morning, he said, "Look, Doloré, here I am in Madrid. I liked Madrid, Doloré. Near the Plaza Mayor, there was this Gypsy bar. A dump. But there was an old singer. His face was all wrinkles and he had a voice like a wagon creaking, like horses sliding in mud. It made me feel I was a kid again. When I was little. When we were always traveling and the wagon was crowded and smelly and we were always hungry. I remember, 'cause my mother, she's in Glory now, when she was nursing, I used to suck on my cousin Emilio's little finger 'cause I thought there would be milk.

"Then we heard about Alcalá. My mother was happy and singing 'cause there were caves and we wouldn't have to travel anymore. But when we got there, the caves were black and cold and full of fleas. We lived in mud. So we built fires and sat around them and sang. We had nothing but flamenco."

~

Pio and Aurora grew up breathing the *cante.*

The Gypsies of Alcalá were poets of the night. They recorded their history in song. A flamenco tradition had begun. But it found its apogee not in the *cante* but in the guitar of Antonino, Pio, and Rosario's uncle.

Antonino's star was ascendant until the day he died. For fifty years, he was the dominant flamenco guitarist of Spain, rarely leaving Alcalá.

With his owl eyes and sunken cheeks, he played the guitar every day from three in the afternoon until three the next morning. He played in bars and in the plaza. He played if no one was listening. He played if everyone was listening.

Antonino never courted followers. He never had an agent or a manager. Nor did he ever dream of charging money for his music; it was his art.

Aficionados followed him wherever he went. They talked the excitement of his music—the cool lime sound of jazz fused with the flowery melodies of Islam.

His rhythms and syncopations bounced and trembled after each other. Bending over his guitar in a bar or the plaza, playing the same music over and over, he'd work out a long jazz line. Finding a new truth, he'd hiccup his shoulders once and look up surprised at himself. Then he'd wag his head in pleasure and smile at the *aficionados* sitting sideways in their chairs, listening to him with their whole bodies.

Antonino walked white through the streets of Alcalá, his guitar always in his arms. To eyes already seeking, his was an air of holiness.

In the sixties, flower children on their way to India from San Francisco took time out in Alcalá. The Gypsies accepted them. They saw in the barefoot, bedraggled hippies—hated by the Spaniards—a commonality.

And for the flower children, Alcalá had music and a guru.

They would sit on the curbs with their feet in the gutters, their guitars in their laps, listening to Antonino, eager for one word of instruction. Antonino would play for them, smile from his monk's place, then walk away.

In his lifetime, he took only three students, his nephews— Patricio, Joaquin, and Rosario. Patricio and Joaquin were brothers; Rosario, was their *primo hermano*, first cousin.

The three nephews were raised on the guitar.

Patricio's playing was brilliant, expert. His cold technique sprayed stars; he cast no shadows. As well as virtuosity, his sleek head, white cuffs and manicured nails brought an elegance and a formality new to the flamenco guitar.

Joaquin, his younger brother, was romantic, languorous. His music was the Alhambra by moonlight.

For Patricio and Joaquin, Antonino's music went straight

into their blood.

Rosario, however, did not wait on anyone's influence. Not even Antonino's. Rosario's art was impolite. He found new intonations that shocked the ears. If Antonino's sound was cool lime, Rosario's was the fleshy olive. One taste filled the mouth, both sweet and stinging.

Some said Rosario went even further than Antonino, left him behind. Rosario's playing was percussive, erratic, disturbed; it rattled the spirit. But it was also exhilarating.

He was to be the successor to Antonino—or so he thought.

Many flamencos tout themselves as someone's 'successor.' Old flamencos, before they die, often do name someone who carries on their particular style of flamenco. But not Antonino. Once, however, he did say that Patricio had the *afición*—both the passion and the discipline. Patricio's family twisted the words until they said 'successor.'

~

In the little car, advancing towards Alcalá, Rosario was babbling in fast forward, "You'll see, Doloré. You'll see when we get to Alcalá. Patricio says he is the successor to Antonino. I tell you, Doloré, I am Antonino's successor!"

As for myself, I wasn't caring who succeeded whom. The gears were arguing with every hill. I held my breath every time I shifted.

Rosario, who couldn't drive a car or even fill a tank, was oblivious to my problems—and to my own expectations around his trip.

In California, he had told me all he would do for me in Spain—introductions, he would take me around to meet all the 'real' flamencos, the *puros*. More than that, he would give me perspective

76

on what I was doing with Pio, help me with the hard places in Pio's choreography.

But in the car, he was talking only about himself. "You'll see, Doloré. You'll see tonight at the *festival*. (The *festival* was news to me.) It will be like when Antonino was alive, Doloré. All the flamencos, the important flamencos, they will be there. And they will all know me."

Once, all the flamencos had known him. It was true. Among the thousand mediocre flamenco guitarists in Andalucía, and the hundred good ones, Rosario had been the new hope. While still in his teens, his black hair in curls to his shoulders, an entourage of thick-jowled managers and agents had paraded him like a bullfighter through the streets of Alcalá and Sevilla.

All the bookings, all the connections, were pre-arranged. Pio had a poster on his wall of Rosario looking young and eccentric in a pink suit, guitar in his hands, ready for his first major concert.

But Tanya, a flower child, showed up in Alcalá. If neither Joaquin—quiet and sensitive—nor Patricio—cool and self-possessed—were Tanya's idea of a Gypsy, Rosario was.

While everybody else was following Antonino, Tanya was following Rosario. They married, and Rosario took his guitar and his talent to northern California.

12

EL FESTIVAL

It was the tragedy of Rosario that he ever left his clan. He had no talent for adapting. He found only chaos in freedom: his marriage to Tanya, of five years and three children, was over; his current relationship with Morningstar was going sour; his career was going nowhere.

In California, those students close to Rosario became his Spain, his clan. "My Gypsy family," he called us. We came together in the evenings in the tiny apartment he shared with Morningstar. Out of a makeshift kitchen, she would bring her sloppy salads, Rosario, his bean stews, always burned on the bottom. There was bread; there was wine.

We would sit squashed together around a card table. One bump of the knees and it would tip. We'd giggle; Rosario laughed with us.

He was warm and generous. Raucous and funny. He'd dance after dinner, twisting and turning his pudgy torso, thick as a frog's, whipping his short legs around each other. In his excitement, he'd pull his cheeks off their bones, pop and roll his eyes, flash his bright chipmunk teeth.

Or he'd be serious. Playing the guitar, singing, his music roamed Andalucía for us. We basked in its sunlight, smelled its olive soaked land, saw the totem shadows on cave walls.

We who were close to him sang his genius. He was our

rainbow guru. Other students who came and went saw Rosario with colder, wiser eyes. But we ignored his breaks with reality, his black rages, and his drinking.

The same energy that propelled his genius was driving him into dark corners. It was obvious in California—to everyone but us—that his gift of hands and voice was declining as his drinking was increasing.

But Rosario lied easily, unconsciously, dreamily, as if composing music. Caught in a lie, he was never embarrassed; another one came along to take its place. The biggest lies were always the ones he told himself.

And the biggest of those? That he could return to Spain and it would all be the same again.

~

Between the gears and Rosario's mood, it was a long, tense morning.

The closer we got to Alcalá, the more agitated Rosario became. Sweat broke out over his upper lip. "Patricio," he said, "he knows I'm better than he is. He plays cold as a stone. Joaquin, he's as weak as a woman."

I didn't say anything.

"I play what Antonino taught us, Doloré. But I do different things too. Patricio and Joaquin, they never go outside of Spain. They do nothing different. All they do is copy Antonino. But me! I copy nobody! And they hate me, Doloré, 'cause they know I'm the best."

A turn in the road and I headed, gratefully, for Alcalá.

"I'll get dressed up," Rosario went on, "And I'll get my father dressed up. You too, Doloré. You get dressed up. We'll go to the *festival* in a taxi. We'll arrive big. It'll all be the same again.

They'll all come around to see me. The important flamencos!"

By this time I was getting tired of the "important flamencos." Besides, I was hearing Pio, the same inflections in the same words— my first inkling that Rosario might be mostly talk, might not make good on his promises.

He kept talking, but I was only listening with one ear. With the other, I was hearing my heart beat harder. "Then tomorrow," he said, "we'll spend all day with my father. 'Cause he's old."

"*Sí,* 'cause he's old," I said.

"And I want you to see Constancia's new flat, Doloré."

"I've already seen it," I muttered.

"Then I'll introduce you to all the flamencos, the real ones. I'll talk you loud to them, Doloré. And when we get back to Sevilla, I'll watch you in Pio's studio."

Now these words I wanted to hear. I relaxed and let myself believe Rosario.

~

Driving into Alcalá was like driving through a flower, white in the sun, blue in the shadows.

At the *pensión,* I let Rosario out and parked where I could pull out—frontwards. I checked in with Nemesio. Rosario said he was going straight to his father's house.

My room in the *pensión* was clean, sparse, with a mattress like packed grass, one lightbulb hanging from the ceiling, and a bathroom—because I was American.

Tired out, I slept the siesta, then changed into my dress— wrinkled—and walked up the hill to Rosario's family home. I walked in on a scene.

Constancia and Benita were getting the old man ready to go to the *festival,* Rosario's 'gift' to him.

The sisters had Teo in a large galvanized tub in the middle of the living room. They were pouring in the hissing, spitting water straight from the stove. While Teo was shivering from his waist up and screaming about his "waist down," I was sitting in a corner wishing I had something small to do, like sewing on a button.

Once Teo was out of the tub, dripping and shrunken, his daughters dressed him in his good blue suit, the one he wore for his wife's funeral, while Rosario called a cab.

In the taxi, old Teo protested; he wanted nothing more than to be home in bed. I protested too, silently. Rosario reeked of cologne; the driver just reeked. Four of us in a taxi the size of a Fiat.

We arrived at the *festival* barely on time, but there was still a big crowd out front. Rosario had indeed gotten dressed up. He wore a black suit and a cherry red shirt with big white polka dots. Smiling at everyone, his face was shining.

Only two little boys with scuffed knees who were standing in the gutter noticed him. "Are you one of the singers?" they asked. Rosario said yes.

The *festival* was being held in the patio of an orphanage. We had a long corridor to walk, old Teo hobbling on his crutches, me on one side of him, Rosario on the other, his eyes everywhere except on his father. People passed us. Rosario's smile was loud. But no one said anything to him.

The tables were almost full. We found seats at the end of one. The old man and Rosario were not acknowledged. And being in the company of Gypsies, neither was I.

Nor was there any recognition from the stage that one of Antonino's nephews was in the audience. No one called Rosario up to play; no 'important flamencos' approached him.

For Rosario, *again* was not happening. His solution was the well-stocked bar at the back of the patio.

If I was uncomfortable in the taxi, it was nothing to how I was feeling after Rosario left the table. The old man sat and said nothing. His eyes were deep in their sockets, his mouth falling in on empty gums. I tried to talk to him. Suddenly he could only understand *Caló*. His eyes began to water. Then he roared a sound; it could have been a word, I wasn't sure. But I was sure there was agony in his voice.

I went back to the bar and found Rosario talking up his successes in San Francisco to a group of men. I interrupted, "Your father's unhappy. You'd better come to the table."

"Can't you handle him, Doloré?" he responded. "I'm busy."

"Rosario, you'd better come back to the table. You'd—"

Rosario stopped me, "Doloré, this isn't California. You don't talk to me when I'm with a group of men. A woman doesn't tell me when to come and when to go."

I was stunned. And embarrassed in front of the ring of men, their faces showing nothing. I had walked right into the *machismo*. It wouldn't be the last time.

I didn't speak; I glared. Rosario glared back. But he turned, left the bar, returned to the table, and gathered up the old man under the armpits like a crumpled coat. Hurriedly, he walked him out of the patio down the long corridor, Teo hopping on his one leg, me coming from behind with the crutches.

I stood and watched as Rosario got Teo into a taxi and shoved money into the driver's hand.

Then Rosario went back to the bar. I went back to the table, completely deflated, only half-aware of what was happening on the stage.

But it didn't matter. The evening was colorless and plodding.

The *festival* was the last of a long circuit. After all the minor cities and many major ones, the best flamenco singers, dancers, and guitarists in Andalucía were tired.

By midnight, the talking and laughing in the audience was drowning out the performers.

Patricio was the only light. He put to shame the half-hearted efforts of his compatriots whipping out yards of music without excitement.

After the last set, Patricio came out into the audience to applause and back-slapping. Smiling, he walked back to the bar. I followed him. My embarrassment had turned to anger at Rosario. I wanted to exact payment. I was going to make a cool demand that he introduce me to Patricio.

But I stopped a few feet from the bar. No Rosario.

~

I walked back alone to the *pensión*. When I arrived, Rosario was out front with a little coterie of men he had trailed from the *festival*. Seated on the curb, they listened as he stood damning Patricio's music as "cold," "dead," and worst of all "not *puro.*"

But Rosario's face was unlit by any power; no one was fearing his opinions. Least of all Patricio, who I heard had left the *festival* with a large group of *aficionados* following him. In an old country inn, he played out the energy still in him until the next afternoon.

Listening to Rosario rant on the sidewalk, I waited, hoping for something from him that would explain his treatment of me, and of his father. Nothing. Shivering, I went into the *pensión*.

~

It was dawn before I fell asleep. Then I slept longer than I intended. At eleven I went looking for Nemesio to check out.

Rested, I felt forgiving, even sympathetic towards Rosario. The *festival* had been a catastrophe for him.

Nemesio was in his 'office,' a space under the staircase just big enough for a desk. He said his *muy buenos* and handed me my complimentary breakfast—coffee and a stale dinner roll.

He knew all about the *festival*, although he hadn't been there. I didn't have to ask how he knew. Nemesio sat outside his *pensión* at a card table every day, all day. As long as Alcalá had Nemesio, it didn't need a newspaper.

"I'm checking out," I told him. "And then I'm going up to Teo's to meet Rosario."

"He's gone, Doloré." Nemesio responded, "He went back to Sevilla on the morning bus."

"Gone? I don't understand."

"*Sí*, Doloré. Before dawn, I saw him walking down the middle of the street like a rag man with his hair all over his head. He was drunk. He was crying."

"Oh my God."

"*Sí*, Doloré. 'Cause Patricio, he was a big success at the *festival*. And nobody knew Rosario was even there. 'Cause, well, I'm not saying anymore, Doloré."

"But we came here just so he could be with his father before—"

"*Sí*, before the old man really up and dies. But I tell you, Doloré, Rosario says it is Patricio who is cold. I tell you, it is Rosario. He missed even his own mother's funeral. But I'm not saying anymore."

And he didn't.

~

Back again in Sevilla, I called Rosario. He was living at

Pio's flat. Was he all right?

"*Sí*, but nobody talked to me at the *festival*. Nobody called me to play. I'm going to leave Spain, Doloré. I want to leave right now. But I can't. 'Cause Morningstar, she bought my airline tickets and she messed up, I have to stay longer."

"How long?"

"I don't know. Longer. A couple of months."

"When will I see you, Rosario?"

"We'll see each other, Doloré. Sometime. When I can."

I hung up the receiver feeling ill. The *festival* had been a disaster for Rosario. Now he was a disaster happening on me—none of the excitement around his trip, none of the entrees to the sacred spaces of flamenco. And none of the help with Pio's choreography.

Whatever I had to do, I would have to do it by myself.

For the first time, I felt alone in Spain.

· 13 ·

LA EXTRANJERA

I had been back from Alcalá three weeks when Manolo came up to my apartment again. It was a Saturday, no Pio—relief. I sat barefoot, spreading my toes in the air. My door was open.

Manolo stood in the shade of the canvas awning that covered my small terrace. Shade in September was water in the desert. Muslin awnings were spread over Sierpes from one rooftop to another. Pedestrians hugged the shadows of buildings. *Sombrillas*, green window blinds, were draped over balconies creating pockets of deep shade.

I invited Manolo in for a cold drink, but he said no with a shake of his head. Gypsies either talk a blue streak, like Rosario, or hardly at all, like Manolo. With no warming to his topic, he said, "Aurora, she wants you to come to dinner."

Dinner in Sevilla is two p.m. It was two p.m.

I was learning. I did not ask, "Now? Who else is coming? Can I bring something? Do I have time to change?"

I grabbed my keys, after shoving my feet in shoes reluctantly.

Not that I didn't want one of Aurora's meals. Her gazpacho was always served tepid, country style. No iciness masked its flavors—cucumber that burst cool in the mouth, "just enough" tomato, sweet green pepper that cracked on the tongue, onion like the bite of a flea. Eaten with thick, aromatic bread that Aurora had made with her own heavy hands.

Her fried fish, crisp and thin as rice paper on the outside; inside, each flake separated cleanly. For desert, a flan that coated the mouth with caramel before slipping evenly down the throat.

Before dinner, *tapas*: *ensalada rusa* (potato salad), *pulpitos* (deep-fried, thumb-sized octopus eaten like popcorn), *tortillas* (small potato and onion omelets) rimmed with threads of golden olive oil.

~

At the door to the flat, Aurora took me by the elbow and gently steered me to her kitchen. I caught a glimpse of Pio lying on the living room sofa.

Aurora and I ate the big meal of the day on a wobbly card table.

Her exquisite cooking left me in no mood for distractions. But Aurora wanted to talk. "*No tiene remedio*," she kept saying, "*no tiene remedio*."

"What can't be fixed?" I asked.

"Rosario," she sighed. Even Aurora, who tolerated much in the name of family, was upset with Rosario.

"Doloré," she went on. "I asked Rosario and everybody. I told everyone to come. Oh, *sí*, I got some good fish and chicken, and I made a big paella. And everybody came, Doloré. Everybody but Rosario!"

Tired of Rosario, I changed the subject. "Pio," I asked, "he's not eating?"

Aurora tapped her temple with her fingertips. "*Que pena. Que pena*," she murmured.

"He's sick? He has a headache? From where the horse kicked him?"

"Oh, no, Doloré. No horse ever kicked Pio. Oh, no, it was that Guardia who—"

But Aurora stopped herself mid-sentence, clamped her lips shut; her cheeks turned white.

"Pio wasn't kicked in the head by a horse?" I said. I was incredulous after months of being told by Pio how he had gotten his scar at *Feria*, how he hated horses, how he had tried to ride one anyway. ("And I got my reward," he would add.)

I waited on Aurora, thinking she'd explain herself. But Aurora sat silent, looking down at her hands like a naughty child.

I changed the subject. "Aurora, you know Heike? You know who she is?"

Aurora without looking up said, "Heike? The German woman? *Sí*. I know her. Her house, it's near here. Where everybody always goes. Except me and Pio. 'Cause we're not welcome."

Oh, God, I thought, I've only made things worse.

~

Rosario was becoming a receding reality to me. He drifted away with only a wave of his hand at a distance. I was stung by his indifference. But I have him to thank for meeting Heike.

Rosario had been seen strutting in this bar and that, forcing his relic humor on anyone who would listen, his laughter as empty as wind chimes wrapped in paper.

A few nights before Aurora's dinner, Rosario and I were in the same bar at the same time. I didn't think he knew I was there.

He was standing with a group of Spaniards, talking in his high monkey voice. Middle of a word, wine glass in hand, he ran out to the street. I watched through a window as his drink sloshed on the pavement.

He's gone nuts, I thought.

He waved down a white car with his empty glass, then stood in the middle of the street talking to the driver. A couple of minutes later, he came running back into the bar. "Doloré!" he yelled, "that was Mariano! We're going over to Heike's!"

"Heike?" I said.

I had roamed the *barrios* at night with other flamencos listening for a guitar or *cante* coming from a patio, or a *juerga* we might crash. Across the river in Triana, we looked for someone dancing in the back room of a bar. We had walked the banks of the river to hear Gypsies singing. But I had never heard of Heike's house.

"Heike who?" I asked as I left the bar with Rosario with no words of protest, no memory of my shredded feelings.

At the white car, Rosario introduced me to Mariano through the window, a lean line of a man with a soft round face. From Rosario's tone of voice, I felt I should have known who he was. I should have.

A few nights later I heard Mariano play a concert in the patio of a fifteenth century monastery outside Sevilla.

He was supposed to have played with the Yugoslavian Symphony. But somebody in city hall forgot to send them the plane tickets. So he played alone to 500 people—without amplification. None was needed; there was no noise in that audience. When he played "Recuerdos de La Alhambra," his trills rippling like water, even the ghosts of the old monks were listening.

But in the car, I had little chance to find out more about Heike or Mariano. Rosario did all the talking. In a five-minute ride, he filled in his "almost four weeks" in Spain. Mariano responded, his English limited to three phrases: "Oh my God!," "How about that?," and "Oh shit," spoken like a benediction.

Mariano drove through a maze of black back alleys, then turned onto Calle del Alba. He parked at a small plaza with blank houses and barred windows. No faces. No sounds. A street lamp that lit up only itself.

We walked across the bleak plaza to old, double wooden doors; Mariano yanked at a clanking cowbell.

A moment's wait, and Heike opened the doors and welcomed us in her gritty Spanish.

~

"*La Extranjera*" she was called by the Sevillanos, 'the foreigner,' although she had lived forty-five years in Spain, twenty of them in Sevilla.

She had freckles rising to a cock's comb of red hair, a bony, narrow face, and a slim body with boyish breasts, small lanterns in a dark night.

A German Jewess, her family had believed Hitler's threats and fled to northern Spain. After the war, Heike taught German and moved slowly south, one city after another, never satisfied until she reached Sevilla. In its ancient culture, and the Gypsies' wide humanity, she found solace and flamenco.

She knew she would never leave.

Putting one *duro* next to another, she bought an old house. It had been a *vecindad* of a clan of Gypsies. Big rooms opened onto the patio, each housed one large family. Upstairs, a long wooden balcony, more rooms, more families.

In a narrow hallway off the balcony, the Gypsy women had cooked on small iron boxes over open fires. There was no gas. No electricity. No plumbing. Only a fountain in the patio for water. Everyone, dogs and horses included, drank from it; everyone bathed in it.

When even the Gypsies abandoned the *vecindad,* Heike moved in and piece by bit, by herself, pushed back the rubble. She built walls, laid tile, put in plumbing and electricity. She made the ruin into a space for her life—and for flamenco.

~

Heike ushered us out of the darkness of the plaza into her living room, glowing like the blossom of a cholla cactus. In the yellow blur of its petals, people moved in soft circles, their faces reflecting the luminescence of low lamps.

Heike moved among her guests with frisky elbows, knobby knees, and low laughter. There was a comfortable mess of cigarette smoke, wine, and *tapas.* And layer upon layer of guitar music: Pablo de Córdoba, the accompanist loved by singers, his big banana hands playing a *Guajiras,* guided us from Spain to Cuba.

Joaquin played, not with the splendor of Patricio's technique, nor with Rosario's fire, but with a deep sweetness and a lilt, like children running through a rainbow.

And Mariano. Sitting or walking, the guitar was never out of his arms. He played the classical composers: Rodrigo, Ponce, Sor, Torrega. And flamenco—in a dozen different styles.

The evening moved gently from inside to outside.

In the patio, at a rickety little table, all legs different lengths, I sat with Lise. Olive skinned with an arched nose and cheekbones like ledges, she could pass for Gypsy. But she was born and raised in London. She left there to study with Pio, and live with Joaquin.

Lise was the dark thread I would come to love. She smiled often, yet a smile seemed foreign to her. There was a sadness about her as clinging as the scent of oranges. She attracted me; I wanted a quiet friend between myself and the Gypsies. Within two weeks, Lise and I were deep friends.

In candle-time, Lise and I watched shadows on the walls and Heike's Siamese kitten chasing lizards under the bougainvillea.

That first night, I also met Leonarda and Marta, sisters, Gypsies, well-known singers. Leonarda, shy, hung around Heike like her shadow and spoke only to her. Marta, robust and loud, spoke to everyone but remembered no one. "Oh, you're from California?" she asked me three times that night.

Pablo, Mariano, Joaquin, Leonarda, Marta—these were the Gypsies. But then there were the *payos*, like myself. "Clowns" the Gypsies call the non-Gypsies. I didn't mind.

Fedro. He came to Sevilla to study flamenco guitar. He had a halo of fuzzy graying hair and a gap in his lower front teeth where he stuck his cigarette so he could smoke while he played.

There was Bartolo, a Bolivian-born dancer who every year spent six months laying bricks in San Francisco and six months dancing in Sevilla.

Michael, also from California, who began calling himself "Miguel" the day he arrived in Madrid. He planned to spend the rest of his life in Spain studying the guitar.

Heike had a sure touch for picking people—none of the hard-edged types, none of the commercial theatricals, none of the lunatic fringe. And none of Rosario.

The only dissident note in the evening was Rosario having an argument with Heike in the hallway. Rosario, his vowels rolling, "Then you're no longer my friend, Heike!"

Heike, all sparks in the consonants, "We were never friends, Rosario."

Rosario left, slamming the double wooden doors. He was never at Heike's again.

Pio was never at Heike's, either. On the other hand, he was

never absent. Constantly talked about, his foibles were laughed at, his troubles sighed over.

Except for his scar. The big joining place where surgeons had put his skull back together. After Aurora's revelation, I asked questions. My words died in the air. Among the Gypsies, there were mysteries—mysteries and secrets—kept either by silence or elaborate subterfuge. But I had never asked the Gypsies to be commonplace; I wanted them mysterious.

~

At three in the morning, Lise and Joaquin walked me the six blocks to my apartment.

At ten in the morning, I had my lesson with Pio. I danced like a rag. I told Pio I had been out late (I didn't say where). Pio looked at me with disgust. "Well, what do you expect if you stay up all night?"

But that night, and most nights, I was back at Heike's.

· 14 ·

LA AMERICANA

The Spanish word for woman is *mujer*.

If the final *'r'* is rolled—*mujerrr*—it refers to the beauties seen on the streets, the long-limbed, dusky-skinned, doe-eyed young women.

If the final syllable is whispered—*muje*—it is referring to the young matrons with crimson-winged mouths, dressed in black velvet at Holy Week, walking four abreast. According to Lorca, "[they]... carry the words, 'long live Sevilla!' in their *mantillas.*" In summer, these women wear pastel chiffons. In fall, red and blue plaid, a background to the gold threads of Sevilla.

But if the word *mujer* is in the plural—*mujeres*—and said with a slight smile, then one is talking about the army of dumpling-bodied, round-spirited, little middle-aged ladies on stumpy legs who carry string bags of groceries by day and dance the *Sevillanas* by night.

Pedestrians move aside for them; bus drivers make extra stops for them; bartenders give them free drinks; police carry their bags.

It is said the *mujeres* run the city, that they hold together the whole of Sevilla with their chain of gossip.

~

Off the boulevard by the department store, down the short alley and to the right was the used clothing store, its back room for

95

second-hand flamenco costumes, faded, the underarms discolored, the belt lines stiff from sweat.

Several *mujeres* sat in the front room sorting the newest used clothes, going through each garment carefully, feeling for anything that didn't belong, maybe a coin. The women talked as they worked, their ideas close to home—their children, their husbands, their cooking, their shopping. The women never stopped talking; they all talked at once.

They didn't speak to me. But as I walked back to the flamenco room I would hear them: "*La Americana,*" they would say, meaning me, "she comes from California. She's not a *jipi* (hippie). But she has the Gypsies for friends. She is here to study flamenco from that awful little Pio. She is here for a year."

I didn't mind their gossip; it was like a warm sheet on a cold night, an inclusiveness that bent its weight to me. Still, if they knew I was going to be a year in Sevilla, they knew something I didn't. My only plan was to stay in Sevilla until either my patience with Pio, or my money, ran out. Whichever came first.

Every day, Pio pushed me through the *Alegrías* and the *Siguiriyas,* demanding speed, accuracy, and polish. I could never accomplish all three at the same time. And I wanted him to start on the *Soleá.* I was getting anxious. It was only October, and already my money was dwindling—so was the rate of exchange. Each lesson, I asked Pio when he would begin the *Soleá.* And each lesson, he responded, "*Cálmate, Doloré.* There's no hurry. I'm the best teacher in the whole world! I know what I'm doing."

~

There was no regular guitarist for my lessons. Guitarists would wander into Pio's studio, play for one lesson, and I'd never see them again. I never knew from one morning to the next if there would be a guitarist at all. Or simply Pio banging his cane and calling the counts.

I wanted to dance to the full voice of flamenco: the *cuadro*—guitarists, *palmeros*, and singers. Without them, the dancer is only a shadow on the stage. But I would have been satisfied to start with just a good guitarist, if I could afford one.

Fedro said he would play for me free for the experience. Pio told Fedro he would have to pay *him* for the privilege of playing in his studio. Fedro said no.

Julio, Pio's nephew, a fine guitarist, had come into the studio once or twice and played for me. A young Greek god—Pan—he had a large straight nose that started from between his eyebrows, shiny black olive eyes, a mass of curly hair. He had just married his first cousin, Consolación, and he was looking for work.

Pio asked me one morning to hire Julio on a daily basis. I told Pio I would love to but I was in a panic over money—the dollar had dropped ten points overnight. Pio said nothing until the end of the lesson. Then he invited me for a drink that night at the Bar Jimenez.

Pio invite me for a drink? At the Bar Jimenez? I should have known better.

The Bar Jimenez was right down from my apartment and around the corner. It was a men's bar. I knew where I could go, where I couldn't. But I dropped my defenses and trusted, of all people, Pio.

When I entered the bar, Julio and Pio were already there. I guessed Julio was paying for the drinks. They came over to me casual, smiling. Handed me a *vino verano*, casually. We talked, casually. I was not aware that they were moving me towards a corner of the bar—until my back hit hard against the wall.

Then they started, faces right up to mine, mouths shrieking words, first Pio, then Julio, "You must hire Julio!" "You will hire me!" "Hear Julio." "Hear Pio. Listen to him!"

All I could reply was, "No! No, I won't! No, I can't. No!"

I tried to move away. But Pio put an arm across my shoulders, pinning me into the corner. I remember anger rising to my chest with such force I thought my ribs would break. This time I had no shoe in my hand to hurl. But my physical strength was well-honed. I swung out both my arms, caught Pio and Julio in the mid-sections, and knocked them off balance.

Then I ran, out of the bar, around the corner, up five flights, and into my apartment.

I wanted to pack it all up and go home. The hell with Pio; the hell with flamenco; the hell with Rosario for getting me into this. And while I was at it, the hell with Spain. The other men in the bar had seen what happened and done nothing. Where was the famous Spanish chivalry? The *pundonor*?

Winded and trembling, I yanked a suitcase out of the closet and began throwing in my clothes, starting with my flamenco skirt and shoes. But the steam went out of me quickly. I sat down on the edge of my sofa, crying for lost causes everywhere. And went to bed early.

~

In the morning, Sevilla had gone cold to me. I awoke asking myself how quickly I could get it together to leave. Go to the Iberia office, go to the bank, send telegrams.

Too early for anything to be open, I dressed and walked over to Heike's, hoping she would be up, hoping for sympathy.

She met me at the door in her bathrobe—she hadn't been to bed yet—gave me a cup of coffee and a *churro* to dunk. She sat listening to my story, her head cocked to one side.

If I wanted sympathy, I got it, German style.

"So," she said when I finished, "now you know why I won't let the little rat-faced bastard in my front door. And Julio's no better. What else do you want me to say? You already knew what Pio's like. Did you go to him so he could be nice to you? Is that why you study with him?"

"No. Of course not."

"Then what's your problem?"

"Heike, you don't understand. My money's tight right now. And Pio wants—"

"You Americans!" she interrupted. "You've got more money than all the rest of us put together and still that's all you think about. Quit thinking about money. You came here for flamenco. If you don't have your own guitarist, you'll never be an artist. You need to work out the music with someone. You should have a singer, too. Joaquin's sung for you a couple of times?"

"*Sí.*"

"What was it like, Doloré?"

"Like heaven."

"So now you know flamenco, how it can feel. But flamenco's deep, Doloré, a lifetime. Whatever you take back to the States will be only a portion of it. But take back as much as you can. Don't let Pio beat you down."

I listened to Heike. I thought about hiring Julio. It might mean I'd have to leave Spain early. If I did, at least I would leave with a whole portion.

Later in the morning, I walked over to the studio. It's hard to stay angry in Sevilla. Warm sunlight was enclosing me in October. The air was thick and smelled of oranges, saffron, and fresh *churros* being fried. Small, noisy birds were flying in and out of a stork's nest on a church roof. The Thursday flea market was being set up in the street. Someone was singing de Falla in full voice.

I went to the studio intending to tell Pio that I would hire Julio. It wasn't necessary. Julio was already there, his guitar balanced across his lap, waiting for me.

~

Mornings with Julio. He was condescending but available.

My feelings wanted to forget what had happened in the bar; my mind wouldn't. But I needed Julio right then, even more than Pio. After my lessons, and whenever Pio ran out for a beer, Julio would work with me. I was learning.

Pio had changed my lessons from ten a.m. to eleven. Lise was now taking the first hour. Joaquin played for her. I came early to watch her, listen to Joaquin, and do *palmas* for them. And they stayed on to do the same for me.

Within a week of hiring Julio, I was dancing in a *cuadro*. All four voices: Pio and Lise, *palmeros*, clapping in counterpoint to each other; Joaquin singing the *Alegrías* as no bird ever sang joy; Julio improvising on the melody. And me, my heels a red thread winding through the other voices.

Like beads on embroidery that catch the light, the accents of the *compás* have to fall in just the right places.

Flamenco is jazz. *Compás* is its touchstone; it holds a *cuadro* together. The words 'out of *compás*' strike terror in a flamenco's heart.

Time and again, I would get 'out.' My mind would turn to mush. I couldn't find my own feet. The *cuadro* would end in confusion. Joaquin would stop singing. That wonderful voice and I couldn't dance to it. Julio, disgusted, would light up a cigarette. Pio would stare at me blank-faced.

Joaquin came up to me after one lesson and said he understood my difficulties. One thing had to be added at a time, he said. I was overwhelmed, he said. I shouldn't be in a hurry.

But with my money problems, I was in a hurry. My worries rained down on me, stinging like salt. My mornings were only getting worse. I felt I'd never be able to dance in a *cuadro*.

But at night, there was Heike's with Mariano strolling through her house like a troubador, playing with ease, as if a divine wind and not his own hands were working the strings.

And when the night was getting old and I was softening, he would play for me and I would dance. He made the difficult easy. A matter of no fear. I danced like a child skipping to music.

"Doloré has a good ear," he would say to anyone listening. These words from him and I slowly mastered *compás*. And gained confidence.

Pio could see the difference in me. "See, see, *mi alma*," he'd say in my mornings, "I told you I knew what I was doing!"

· 15 ·

Having my lesson an hour later meant I could stay at Heike's until three every morning. Sitting outside in her patio, I didn't even need a sweater in the warm October air.

Nobody warned me about November.

~

Overnight, Sevilla turned from an oven to an icebox.

Rain poured down on my 'apartment,' a three-room stucco cubicle on the roof of a five-story apartment building. I had a front room with a sofa bed, a tiny bathroom and, in the kitchen, a stove, a washing machine, and a fridge which defrosted itself all over the floor.

My kitchen window overlooked the roof of a fifteenth century church with enough accumulated dirt to grow a fig tree. On the roof was a deep stork's nest which also housed bats, swifts, owls, and mice.

From my terrace, barely larger than a footprint, I could see the second city of old Sevilla, a landscape of interlocking roof tops with clotheslines criss-crossing like the web of a maniac spider. Each rooftop had its small, white-washed cubicles like mine. Each had its slanted tile roof, its own garden, and its own *toldo*, a canvas awning that trapped enough shade for tiny black bats, three inches long and thin as pencils, to hang under by day.

I could have walked across the roof-tops to the river. A

thief's heaven, there were six locks on my front door. Inmaculata had put them there.

Inmaculata was my landlady. I called her 'Mack.'

A hefty lady, gold teeth and bleached hair flashing, she bristled, taking to the streets and bellowing orders at her sons like a tank commander. Noe took care of her two apartment buildings; Jesús ran her furniture store. Cheap furniture of particle board, including little round tables with a lower shelf to hold a brazier.

At night, I'd often sit with Joaquin and Lise around the burning coals of their brazier, the tablecloth extending out over our laps. We watched TV, ate, talked, and kept warm. One night, I got too warm and put the tablecloth down in front of my knees. It caught fire, everybody slapping at the flames. I was embarrassed. But Lise showed me all the other places where the tablecloth had caught fire.

I will never understand why Sevilla hasn't burned to the ground.

Late in October, Mack took away my big electric fan. I was glad; it blew a gale—in one direction only. But she didn't replace it with a heater. I asked. She looked at me like she didn't understand the word *frio*.

I demanded a heater. She found one, butane.

The little canisters of butane were called *bombones*, as in 'bon bons,' and they were about as effective.

The *bombones* were delivered once a week, and fast. A horse cart came by loaded with the little orange canisters. The driver yelled, and I had about two minutes to grab the used canister, run down five flights of steps, and get a full one.

Three hours used one up. Chilled to the bone unless I stood right in front of the heater, I walked around my apartment wrapped in a blanket.

But Heike's house was warm and dry. I was spending more time there. So were Joaquin and Lise.

Their 'apartment' was four sheds on a rooftop. On the landing at the top of the stairs to the roof was their kitchen: a butane camping stove, a box for dishes, a basin for water, no fridge.

Each of the sheds was a room—bedroom, living room, a bathroom with a shower and a john flushed with a bucket of water.

Lise assured me that living on the roof in summer wasn't bad, even pleasant crossing from shed to shed.

That left the winters. In the rain and the cold, Joaquin and Lise were happy to spend their evenings at Heike's, who wasn't always happy to stay home. Even with a house full of people, she would leave to hear someone singing in a bar, his *cante* competing with the pin-ball machines.

Mariano, Joaquin, Lise, and I would go with Heike. Hoping to hear some Gypsies, we'd walk along the steel blue twist of the river, everyone in woolens and raincoats. Except Lise in chiffon, and no goose bumps. "Hardy," she'd say, "you've got to be hardy to live in Sevilla."

November, the days were gray. But the bars were light and music.

The bars were so many, we were impatient. We'd wait with a bit of wine to warm our time. If there was no *cante*, we'd leave and walk to the next bar, next door. We could always find some old fellow, teetering, who could raise a crow sound. Drinking in Sevilla ran the river high on its banks. Drinking also cut the cord of the rational mind. It was great for flamenco.

As we went from one bar to another looking for flamenco, we'd run into Rosario. Trying to establish a group of *aficionados*, he had a different reason for bar-hopping. But a renegade Gypsy wasn't wanted by the Sevillanos any more than he was wanted by his clan.

Only Rosario's sisters wanted him to stay in Spain.

And Pio—especially Pio.

~

Every lesson, Pio complained to me about Rosario; sandpaper ran in their shared blood.

Early in November, Rosario finally came to Pio's studio to watch me. He and Pio fought, on my time. Pio complained because of the house that Rosario owned outside Alcalá.

"All you want is my money!" Rosario yelled.

Pio yelled back, "Why not? Why not sell the house? Then you and me, we can open a *salón de fiesta* together. We can be rich. And my head will be up again. I will be someone. They will call me `Don Pio' and not `Pio Get Out!'"

"I can't," Rosario replied, "I can't sell it. This woman, she owns half. She lives in New York."

"So? Go see her in New York and talk to her."

"Pio, I don't have her address. It's in a drawer in California."

"So, go back to California and then go see her in New York."

"Pio, New York and California, they're wide apart."

"I thought they were next to each other. Are you sure they're not next to each other?"

"Pio, there's maybe forty states in between."

"Forty!"

"More than forty—forty-eight."

"Rosario. Why so many?"

"Because there just are, Pio. And two more. But they're separate."

"Separate? Like the Basques and the Canary Islands? They

want to separate."

"No, Pio, Alaska and Hawaii. They were already separate. So they joined."

"Rosario. Why? Why would they join after they got separate?"

"They never got separate. They were always separate."

"Rosario! How could they separate if they were already separate? You're confused, Rosario. You'd better stay in Spain where everybody's confused."

"Pio, you only want me to stay 'cause you think I have money."

"But you do. You do! You own that house."

"Pio, shut up."

The argument went on. I got bored, got dressed, got out. Nobody noticed.

I left wondering how Rosario ever managed to buy a house. He didn't know a dime from a dollar. In California it was, "Doloré, how do I write a check?" "Doloré, do I have enough money to pay for my lunch?" "Doloré, the bank says I'm overdrawn. What does that mean, Doloré?'"

But in Sevilla I was lucky. I lived up five flights of stairs. Rosario wouldn't climb them, even as a last resort. The other Americans had him for a house pet.

~

The third week of November, the Americans at Heike's got homesick for Thanksgiving. She couldn't understand what we were fussing about, but she offered her home, and her stove.

Her stove, unlike mine, had an oven. I offered to buy the turkey—not common and very expensive in Spain, until Heike said to me, "My oven's butane, you understand." I understood: the turkey could come out all brown and crisp on the outside and raw and pink inside. I settled for buying the roast chickens in the basement of the local department store.

Heike made a huge pot of sauerkraut. The smell hung in the house half the night. Ellie, a German girl renting a room from her, fried eggplant. Bartolo brought Danish cookies; no bakery in Sevilla had ever heard of pumpkin pie. Everybody else brought wine.

The sauerkraut made our tongues curl; the eggplant squished like wet fungus; roast chickens are not turkey. But we had our Thanksgiving; the Americans were whole again.

~

The end of November, Rosario left Sevilla to return to California. He stopped at Pio's studio and asked me to go with him to the airport. "Maybe there's going to be Guardias," he said, "Maybe they're going to ask me questions." He looked scared. I said yes.

The next morning, I met Rosario at Pio's flat. Diego was there. He offered to go with us. It was barely dawn when we left for the airport.

In the taxi, Rosario was nervous, babbling, "So, I'm leaving, Doloré. Joaquin and Patricio, they're mean to me. And Pio, he's no good. He says he wants me to stay but all he wants from me is money. I won't give him any. And I won't send any more students to him either. 'Cause when you first got here, Doloré, he and Aurora, they should have treated you better. They should have—"

"Well, they were a little strange," I interrupted. "They acted like they never heard of me." I stopped. A small light went on in my head. "Rosario," I asked, "you did write letters for me, didn't you? You said you were going to. You said—"

"Oh, *sí*, Doloré. I wrote for you. I said you were coming. *Sí*.

But Morningstar, she forgot to mail them."

"You mean to tell me I walked right in on Pio and Aurora and your family in Alcalá and nobody knew me?"

"But it was Morningstar, Doloré. She's not reliable. She—"

"Oh, Rosario, shut up!"

Arriving at the airport, I was in no mood to see Rosario off with one last hug. Diego went in with him and returned smiling. "No Guardias," he said.

~

Back in Sevilla, Diego took me out to breakfast. I told him about Rosario's 'letters of introduction.' I said I didn't know whether to laugh or cry. Diego said it was better to laugh.

Later that morning, I went for my lesson with Pio. He was dejected. Sitting in one of his little chairs, looking down at his feet, he sang a *Soleá*:

> Rosario has left; we fought.
> But he is my brother.
> Now the world is old, and I am old.
> I may never see him again.

· 16 ·

SOLEÁ

Pio's sad song was the only lament for Rosario. No other ashes were scattered around his leaving.

Night poured out of Pio's song, a *Soleá*. It was appropriate; the word means 'loneliness.'

Soleá is the mother song of all *cante jondo*; *Siguiriyas* and *Saeta* are variations on it. But where *Siguiriyas* is passionate, and *Saeta*, ecstatic, *Soleá* is somber and melancholic. Subdued, it leaves by the same door that it entered.

Pio's choreography for *Soleá* seemed inevitable, as if no other steps could ever be put to such music. Or such words:

> I must leave Sevilla
> To serve the king.
> The breezes that come through your door
> Are my sighs I am sending you.

or

> Neither the Pope in Rome
> Nor the creator of anguish
> Could endure the pangs of love
> My body suffers for you.

or

> Death came to my bedside
> But did not wish to take me;
> My destiny was not complete.
> On its departure, I began to weep.

I wanted Pio to start the *Soleá*. He seemed stuck in the *Siguiriyas*. I asked him to at least give me a heelwork exercise for the *Soleá*. So he did, a double tapping of the heel like a nervous tic—two beats to a quarter count. And twice as hard to do in cold weather.

After a week of practice, I thought I had it. I showed Pio.

He shook his head, "No, Doloré," he said. "No. You're just hammering nails in the floor. The sound, it has to be like a shiver, loose. Me, Doloré, I used to do this step with four beats to a count!"

I didn't believe Pio and I never accomplished more than the double-tap. But the little tattoo gave an edge of laciness to my heelwork.

~

The music for *Soleá*, like faded roses, called to me. I kept nagging Pio and he finally began choreographing in late November.

Soleá starts with the dancer seated between the guitarist and the singer. The dancer holds the center of the stage. A spiritual rather than physical command of one's place, it is called *sitio*.

Pio explained *sitio*. "*Mi alma*," he said, "the *Soleá* is a walking dance, where you show the audience who you are. *Soleá*, Doloré, it doesn't move far. But it moves deep."

Duende pays the ticket for this long slow dance.

Sitting at the back of the studio, my eyes cast down, hands lightly on my thighs, one leg stretched out like a morning cat ready to rise, I would begin by circling my wrists, rolling the bones; I could hear them cracking. As Pio's frog voice finished the first verse, I would raise my arms until I had wrapped a wreath around my head.

Only then would I rise from the chair, back straight, one thigh muscle doing all the work of lifting my body. And, oh, did I hear from Pio if there was a moment's glitch, catch, or break in the smooth, steady rise.

Walking to the center of the studio, I imagined myself sleek in a black dress moving with the rhythm of silk.

Pio's choreography had elegance and simplicity. For his *Soleá*, I left the downward thrust of the Gypsy woman's dance and returned to the years of ballet still in my body: the long lines of legs and back, the slight arch between the shoulder blades held by a breath, the reach of the head on a long neck, the arms curving gently like a bird's breast.

In the *Soleá*, I found my *sitio*.

And Pio found his—in a chair, looking down at the floor.

He had started the *Soleá* beautifully, and out of the pain of Rosario's departure. But he dissolved into a messy depression. More than the tule fog that could spread over him, and suddenly lift.

He would leave heelwork passages in the *Soleá* incomplete. My mistakes went unheeded. His attention to detail, the discipline of refinement, were not there.

There were days he would choreograph only one new step in an hour's lesson, with none of the usual boasting over his cleverness, his originality.

I missed it. And I missed Pio. Without him to butt my head up against, the studio was empty; I couldn't grab hold of its vacant corners.

I tried guessing at what he had in mind: "Pio, do I move to the left here? Pio, do I do the same thing again? Pio?"

He wouldn't answer. Julio would light a cigarette and wait. I would just stand, my legs shivering under the warmers.

I asked Heike what to do. "So," she said, "the little runt's depressed 'cause he couldn't get his hands on Rosario's money. And he's giving you trouble. Well, what did you expect?"

I expected him to finish the *Soleá*.

I talked to Mariano. "Pio's depressed?" he said. "Well, Spain's depressing. New York is where everything is."

Mariano was no help, so I talked to Julio. "Pay Pio more and he'll give you more steps."

Thanks, Julio.

Finally, I talked to Lise. I should have talked to her first.

I complained, "Pio's giving me one step in a whole hour. I'm thinking of leaving him."

"*Sí*, he's nuts, Doloré. But don't leave him. Nobody can do what he does."

I knew that. The shabby little man could catch the archetypes in a tin cup. He did his dreaming in the caves. Out of darkness, he could bring a numinous *Siguiriyas*. Or an *Alegrías* that was pure joy. But I also knew he wasn't doing anything.

"He'll come out of this," Lise went on. "I'll help you with his choreography," she added.

Bless Lise.

~

Two blocks from Pio's studio was the Juan Torres studio. Mornings, he taught the *Sevillanas* to the little *mujeres* in the *barrio*. Lise and I began spending afternoons in his studio, Mama Torres watching and serving us *manzanilla* tea.

Lise danced by my side, explaining Pio's steps from the hints I was able to give her. Nobody understood Pio's choreography better than Lise. She unscrambled Pio's steps, and where there were gaps in his choreography, she filled in with a step of her own.

Pio would watch me in the mornings doing steps that belonged to Lise and say nothing. This was the measure of his depression. He never allowed anyone else's steps in his studio. Even those that came to me by way of Rosario he considered 'tainted.'

~

The rain continued. It wouldn't rain long in Sevilla, everyone assured me. All Andalucía is in a perpetual state of drought, they said.

Pio's studio, which always smelled, smelled worse. The dampness picked up the fruity odors of stale wine and rotting food on greasy paper plates. Black fur grew in the corners of the ceiling. I danced in a wet envelope.

The second week of December, the rain did stop. Then the cold snapped.

There was no heat in the studio. Dancing, I kept warm. But Julio suffered. Wrapped in scarves and sweaters, every chance he got he'd hunch over his guitar, warming his hands in his armpits. The cold didn't bother Pio. He drank. In summer, forty beers a day to keep cool; in winter, forty to keep warm.

~

Lise was watching my lesson every day as I slowly pulled steps out of Pio. Meanwhile, Joaquin and Julio would sit arguing in buzzing voices over the way the *Soleá* should be played.

On successive days, their buzzing became hissing. Then one morning, snarling. Julio told Joaquin, "I'm the guitarist here and I'll play *Soleá* the way I see fit!"

Joaquin, who had the distracting habit of saying exactly what he thought, responded by telling Julio he could learn from someone better than he was.

Julio said nothing. He slammed his guitar into its case and, trailing a wool scarf and cigarette smoke, stormed out of the studio.

I sighed. Julio was gone; Pio was useless. I had neither

teacher nor guitarist. But without my asking, Joaquin picked up his guitar and started playing for me.

Julio was technically correct. But in Joaquin's hands, the *Soleá* was dust at the heels of a horse, sad and ephemeral, pervasive, but not heavy. All the subtle colors of its melancholy came forward like speech.

My body still remembers the freedom of Joaquin's support. The awkward new steps and the heelwork were put right. They were all there in his music. I could relax.

~

Pio's studio was closing between December 24th and January 7th. The last days before he closed, neither Julio, Joaquin, nor Lise came to my lessons. I was alone with Pio, his depression becoming a slow drain on my energy.

Each of Pio's dances had, in turn, seemed the one most true to me. His *Alegrías* was full of *gracia*, arms repeating in the air the circling pattern of my feet on the floor. His *Siguiriyas* was a call to my blood. But now the *Soleá*, a fluid grace note I so loved, was being tossed aside. I feared it would never be finished.

I hadn't gotten anywhere trying to be persuasive and polite to Pio. So I tried insulting him. "Pio," I asked, "is the *Soleá* too difficult for you? Do you know someone who could finish it for me?"

If I had thrown a firecracker in his face, it would have had the same effect. He came to life in an instant, stood up, threw his cane on the floor, and yelled at me to leave the studio at once!

I hadn't bargained on that. But I wasn't taking it either. As calmly as I could, I said, "Pio. I've paid you two weeks in advance. You owe me two weeks."

"So, Doloré," he replied, "after Christmas, two weeks. Then

116

you leave."

Pio's words were cold and I smarted from them. But his depression, at least for that moment, lifted.

~

The color of that Christmas in Sevilla was orange. With the chill of clear skies, the green fruit turned overnight. Every orange tree on every street was a Christmas platter. Their aroma mixed with the chestnuts roasting on corner stands, soft smoke rising high in the air, while little Christmas lights strung tree to tree prickled the eyes.

The women turned out for the season in red velvet and fine Scotch plaids.

Christmas in Sevilla was old gold. But I still wanted to be in Madrid; I needed to get away from the provinciality of Andalucía.

And from Pio.

· 17 ·

LA NAVIDAD

Thirteen hours on the slow train to Madrid sandwiched between two nuns talking at me, "Child (I was older than they were), pour me my coffee." "Child, find me a pillow." "Child, help me with my bag." "Child,...."

The dark nuns of Spain walk heavy; their black and brown habits hang to the ground. Wide leather belts clank with crucifixes, keys, rosaries, and rabbits' feet. Round as moons, two nuns abreast can fill the narrow back streets of old Madrid.

That drizzly December, I wandered those streets. In the bakery windows, lined in tiny lights, coffee-cake snakes curled up in tins stared back at me with icing eyes. I sampled the *tapas* bars, their long counters loaded with plates of small food.

In the Café Gijón, over white linens, I eavesdropped on the men's *tertulias*, listened in on the old academics arguing over last year's manual of the Castilian language.

Late afternoons, I sat soft in the bars and sipped hot *chocolate*.

~

Madrid: the Prado, thirty-two other museums, two hundred art galleries, twenty-five theatres, a Royal Palace, a Royal Opera House, a University with its own park, a National Library with two million volumes.

But to find myself in Madrid again, I had to keep the tension between its grandeur and its intimacy. I went to the smaller museums: the Joaquin Sorolla—his red velvet house with its big dim studio, the upstairs gallery filled with bright beach paintings.

The Galdiano Museum for the Turners, the Modern Art Museum, one whole wing for the *Guernica*, the Decorative Arts Museum, one hundred antique Christmas creches tucked between blazing yellow and blue Telavera ceramics. The Romantic Museum, dark walls and darker paintings, the guard walking right behind me, turning off and on the lights in each room.

The street of stalls for rare books and prints, somehow dry and immaculate in the rain.

At night, I enjoyed the buildings lit in pale pink and green. The wide boulevards lined in trees strung with Christmas lights (most of them worked), their colors caught in the ice white spray of fountains.

I even admired the Guardias in gray winter uniforms, their capes down to their ankles.

In the soft, dark nights, the shop windows were shiny. Inside, clerks stood like waiting barbers. I bought fans for Lise and Aurora, a fine leather coin purse for Heike, a set of dominoes for Papa Salinas. And for Mama Salinas, a crucifix from the holy store, the ceiling afloat with fat ceramic angels.

Mama and Papa Salinas, bless them, had found a room for me even with their big family in residence for the holidays.

Christmas Day wrapped me in its dreams. After Mass, Mama in the kitchen, tomatoes sizzling and popping in her cast iron frying pan, Papa in the living room, imitating the poses of the white marble goddesses in Retiro Park with his barrel-shaped body. After dinner, there was decorating the tree and exchanging gifts, Mama and Papa graciously accepting my customs.

I was pleased to be with them, and to be only a few short blocks from the Plaza Mayor. A ghostly square, it was walked for centuries by *hidalgos*, saints, poets, inquisitors, kings. And used for bullfights, *auto de fes, festivales.*

Now the Plaza is for outdoor cafés—except Sundays. Sundays are for stamp collectors standing beside their card tables, their hands thin and spiritual, hanging out of frayed suit cuffs.

But at Christmas, the Plaza is for creches. Stalls fill the great space, each selling a piece of the Nativity: a small holy family in a straw shed with the cows and sheep.

An archway on the plaza opens like a keyhole onto the oldest and shabbiest *barrio* of Madrid, a leftover from the seventeenth century. This is where the cave restaurants are, built into the ramparts of the Plaza. Where *Casa Botín,* Hemingway's restaurant, dark with the Spanish gift for darkness, is. This is where the streets of the cutlers, ironsmiths, and master guitar makers are.

And the street named *Amor de Dios*, with its old wooden building of dance studios, the floors as wavy as a storm at sea.

I went in—just to look—and stayed to watch the flamenco classes, dancers going in and out of the studios to the rhythm of money. Fifteen to twenty clean-lipped young ladies in a class, moving like polished stones. Flamenco as a caricature of itself, faces grimacing in unison, hands clawing the air, backs arched to the point of breaking.

Even the *cante* was ear-splitting.

I couldn't see myself there.

Worse, I *could* see myself there, missing Pio, forgiving him everything. And giving anything to be back in his dirty little studio with him beside me pounding his cane.

~

I had planned to leave Madrid January 6th. But, as anxious to get back to Sevilla as I had been to leave, and hoping to resolve things with Pio, I left on the 5th.

In Sevilla, I took a taxi to Heike's house from the train station; she had invited me to stay with her when I got back.

Certain she would offer no insights about my predicament with Pio, I talked to her about other things as we made *tapas* together for Twelfth Night.

A houseful of people. Co-hosting with Heike, I greeted guests at the door, looked into their faces, wondering if I would be seeing them again. Especially Mariano, Lise, Joaquin—so open, so happy to have me back.

Not wanting to think about leaving Sevilla, or seeing Pio the next morning, I decided to play out the spontaneous edge of flamenco. The quickest way was to dip in the *fino*, a dry sherry with the kick of a mule.

I swallowed the night in *fino* and waited for the release.

But all that happened was that the room began to spin.

Seated in Heike's big chair with the green upholstery, I leaned back, "I'm enlightened," I told myself, "I can see the earth's rotations. No one else knows what I know," I said to myself as I watched the ceiling swim. What I didn't know was that I had turned as green as the chair.

And then, Joaquin on one side, Mariano on the other, I was being walked outside to the patio and set down hard on a bench. Lise put something cold and wet on my forehead.

"Take deep breaths," said Joaquin.

"I'll get some coffee," said Mariano.

"If you're going to throw up, do it here!" said Heike, putting a waste paper basket beside me.

But I didn't throw up; I cried.

~

I sat on the edge of the bed remembering, all too clearly, the night before, Heike and Lise escorting me to Heike's spare room and pouring me into bed. When I awoke, it was well past the hour of my lesson with Pio. My body was so thick and heavy I could barely move. Much less dance.

I put on a robe, went downstairs, and came into Heike's living room embarrassed.

Drunkenness in Spain is contemptible. But getting sick from drinking is ingratiating. Heike had a wide smile and a hug for me, as if I had joined a club.

She handed me coffee and we sat together. Half a mug later, she said, "So, Doloré. What were you crying about last night?"

"Pio, what else?"

"So what happened?" Heike asked.

"I insulted him."

"So? He had it coming. He always has it coming."

"I suppose," I replied, "but I guess I humiliated him. I told him if he couldn't finish the *Soleá*, maybe he knew somebody who could."

Heike laughed and choked on her coffee, "You're lucky he didn't hit you."

"But then he threw me out. Except I'm paid up two weeks in advance. Then I leave. But I don't want to. I've looked around and there's nowhere to go."

"Doloré, you're making this too hard. Just tell the little *sinvergüenza* that you're leaving right away and you want your money back. If he doesn't faint dead on the spot, he'll say you can stay on."

~

I intended to test Heike's advice, but not until Pio finished the *Soleá*.

Returning to his studio the next morning, I leaned on a wish, several wishes, hoping he was over his depression, hoping I could continue with him, hoping Heike was right.

Pio was lighting the votive candles on his altar and straightening pictures on his wall. That was a good sign.

But he said nothing to me. That was a bad sign. I ignored it. I spoke first, no amenities, just, "Can you finish the *Soleá*?"

Pio took a few steps to the center of the studio and stood looking down at his feet. I knew that look: he was choreographing.

"*Sígame, sígame,*" was all he said. I followed him as he danced the last few steps of the *Soleá*. He moved with precision and clarity. I could interpret the new steps at once onto my body. I never felt closer to him as teacher and choreographer.

But whatever rapport I was feeling with Pio, I was the only one feeling it.

I said to him, "Pio, the *Soleá*, it's beautiful. Now, can I dance it all the way through from the beginning? There are some little things I don't understand. I mean I—"

Sarcasm shot out of Pio. "Are the steps too difficult for you?" he hissed. "I can make them easy, simple, Doloré, like for a beginner. Or maybe for you, like a dilettante."

I caught my breath. Then I blew up, "If you want me to leave," I hissed back, "just say so. And what's more, you can keep your dirty little studio. The *Soleá* is done. And I'm done with you!"

I stomped into the dressing room, grabbed my street clothes, and left the studio still in my flamenco skirt and shoes.

~

Halfway up the five flights to my apartment, I realized I hadn't asked Pio for my money back. I wasn't about to.

In my apartment, nothing different. I threw no clothes in a suitcase. Instead, I took a slow shower and ate a long lunch. I was calm; the air had cleared. I was ready for the next move, wherever it might take me.

What I wasn't ready for was a knock on my door.

· 18 ·

CARACOLES

Manolo. He was winded. He had been running. Breath whistling, he said one word, "Aurora."

"What about her?" I asked.

"She wants you."

"Now?" The last place I wanted to be was Aurora and Pio's flat.

"*Sí.* Now. She's sick, very sick."

~

Pio opened the door of the flat. White around the eyes, he stared at me and said nothing, which scared me worse.

Aurora was sitting on the living room sofa propped up by pillows. Her face was red, her breath snorting, her head sweaty. She was patting her chest with both hands and saying over and over, "*Eh normal? Eh normal?*"

I went to her side and put an arm around her shoulders. She leaned her full weight against me. It took all my strength to hold her up. I could feel her body heat through my sweater. She asked again, "*Eh normal?*"

Nothing about her was 'normal.'

Pio and Manolo, one short, one tall, stood in the middle of the room staring at her, mouths open.

I don't know what I expected from Manolo, who spoke only in monosyllables. Or from Pio, who wasn't speaking at all. But I said, as calmly as I could, "A doctor, have you called a doctor? An ambulance?"

No response. Nothing.

Meanwhile, Aurora's body was heaving and pushing against me; my legs were trembling and my arms cramping.

Then the dam broke; Aurora started gasping for air. I was terrified. If I let go of her to go to the phone, she'd fall sideways. I'd never be able to get her up again. Holding her, I yelled at Pio and Manolo, "*Por Dios!* Do something!"

Manolo found his legs and ran to the phone in the kitchen. Pio ran after him.

Pio came back with a bottle of pills and showed it to me.

"What's this?" I yelled at him, "She has pills and you didn't give them to her? Get water."

A jerk moved through Pio's body and he ran back to the kitchen just as Manolo came into the living room saying his one word, "Antonio."

"Oh my God," I said, "I didn't think of him. He's coming? Fast?"

"Fast," replied Manolo.

Pio, running, returned with a cup of water, half-spilled.

My nerves shook, I wasn't sure what was on the bottle—two pills every six hours or six every two hours. I told Pio to put two on Aurora's tongue and get the water down her.

I heard her gullet click. The three of us stood watching her, and waiting. A few seconds and her breathing calmed down. Her body began to support itself.

Voices in the hallway. Antonio came through the door with half the occupants of the building behind him, all giving him advice at once.

Pio and Manolo were shoved aside. One of the women, that angel, came to my side and took over holding up Aurora as the men pushed and pulled her off the sofa.

It took four men, hands crossed under her, to carry Aurora, sitting upright, down the stairs to Antonio's van.

Antonio's 'van' was nothing more than a walk-in wooden box on the back of his pick-up truck; he used it to haul furniture.

Grunting with the effort, the men got Aurora into the back of the van and sat her on a spare wheel on the floor, her 'surplus' hanging over the sides. Diego, who had just arrived, and Manolo crouched beside her and held onto her arms so she wouldn't career off the wheel when the truck moved. Pio, white and shaken but quiet, sat in front next to Antonio.

Antonio took off with a jolt. I watched as he lurched down the street, straddling the curb with two wheels and swerving around pedestrians.

At the hospital, I heard it took Antonio, Manolo, Diego and two attendants to get Aurora off the wheel, onto a gurney, and into Emergency. While Pio, his voice back, walked behind them, complaining loudly about the 'service.'

~

I spent the night walking around my apartment trying to think of things in Aurora's favor. There weren't many.

In the morning, Manolo came up to say she was okay. It was her heart, but she was okay. I wanted to go over to Heike's and bring her up to date, but I realized I was feeling peculiar. I went back to bed to catch up on my sleep, but in a couple of hours it was flu.

Mack brought me extra blankets and *manzanilla* tea, Spanish chicken soup. Lying in the bed, staring at the ceiling, I was thinking about Pio's depression. Heike had said it was because he couldn't get his hands on Rosario's money. I remembered Pio saying after Rosario left, "I am old, Doloré, and I have no money. No money to buy who I was."

But my last lesson with him, he lit all the candles on his altar, crossing himself between each one. Remembering that, and him helplessly watching Aurora, I felt for his littleness.

I wanted to believe his depression was over Aurora's health. Still, I wasn't ready to apologize to Pio.

Nor would it be that simple. Pio, because he didn't acknowledge insults, didn't accept apologies.

~

Aurora was in the hospital two days.

Two of Pio's sisters and five of his nieces came from Alcalá. They stayed at the flat, slept on the floor, tended to Pio's meals, got him back and forth to the hospital, all the time secretly bringing extra food to Aurora, who was hungry again.

Aurora came home with more pills—"They're bigger," she said, "so they'll work better"—and a diet. A week later, I went up to the flat, brought flowers and the fan I had bought her in Madrid. In all the hullabaloo with Pio, I had forgotten to give it to her.

In bed, propped up by pillows, she was so white I thought she would dissolve into the sheets. But she wanted to talk.

"Doloré," she said, "I'm so glad you were here. Pio, he doesn't know what to do. It wasn't just 'cause I was sick that I wanted you here. No. I lied. It was 'cause I wanted you and Pio to patch things up. Sí, Doloré. Pio, he really wants to make it up with you. But he's not going to tell you that. Oh no. But he's got a dance. He's going to tell you he wants to teach it to you. If you say yes, everything will be all right."

~

I was on my way out of the flat when Pio came up to me. "Doloré," he said, "I have a *Caracoles*. It's a pretty dance. You ought to learn it."

Tears were ready behind my eyes. "*Caracoles*?" I asked.

"*Sí*. It's an old dance. And you'll need a fan, Doloré. A big one."

"Tomorrow?" I asked.

"*Sí*, Doloré," Pio replied, "with a fan."

~

The women of Sevilla walk winged, their fans fluttering like young birds in first flight.

A *mujer* may own many fans to match her wardrobe, fans in every color and fabric—fine laces, silks painted with scenes from Watteau or Fragonard, fans with tiny polka dots, fans in bright colors.

The younger the woman, the larger the fan. Adolescent girls spread a wide lace of boned beauty under their early eyes.

The older women 'talk' their smaller fans. In flawlessly measured rotations of the forearm and swift flips of the wrists, their fans imply commas and questions marks, or close with a loud *clack* for exclamation points.

I bought my fan from an *abaniquería*, a fan factory. In a room barely bigger than a closet, a little *mujer* sat at a work table cutting and gluing all day. The finished fans hung from the ceiling like brightly colored bats.

My fan, a flamenco dancer's fan, was turquoise on one side, bright pink on the other. It was bigger and heavier than street fans and less sensitive to tiny impulses of touch.

Pio showed me how to handle it lightly, holding it with only a thumb and ring finger. As if his wrists had no bones. he could wheel the fan in quick circles, at the same time saying, "See, Doloré, the fan goes round and round like the shell of a snail."

~

Caracoles means 'snails.' The Andalucíans say the song gets its name from the *caracoleros,* the street vendors of Sevilla, who hawk the tiny snails, no larger than the end of a finger. While they climb over the sides of the boxes, the vendors sing the beauty of Andalucían women:

> How brilliant become
> the boulevards of Madrid
> when strolled
> by the ladies of Sevilla!

The Madrilenos say the *Caracoles* originated in Madrid. One *cante* for *Caracoles* speaks of the bar, La Union, a bullfighters' hangout in turn-of-the-century Madrid:

> Let us go, let us go
> to La Union,
> where the bullfighters go—
> Cuchares, El Tato, and Leon!

Pio had his own explanation of the origin of the *Caracoles.* "It's pure Gypsy," he said. "Where else would it come from?"

"If you say so, Pio."

~

Pio's choreography for the *Caracoles* was piquant, bright, as if he was shaking off the intense dust of Aurora's crisis. And his own depression.

He came up with a bit of theatrical fun for me, as sprightly as the *zarzuela,* the insouciant teacup operas that spiced up the antique

132

world of Madrid, its graystone formality.

And I made no bones about being a nineteenth century dancer. I was back in the days of old chatter and gentle music in the streets of Madrid.

But Pio's choreography was not simple for being old-fashioned. I circled around and around myself, all the while wheeling the fan as high over my head as I could, or playing it close to my body like a moth to a light.

It was not easy learning to handle the fan. Opening it, Pio wanted to hear only the quiet ripple of the ribs. Closing it, I had one motion with one hand to fold it into a neat bundle. It took a hard snap of the wrist. The first few times I tried, it landed at Pio's feet, splayed out on the floor like a dead bird. Pio was not amused.

Also, as usual, he wanted speed. My nightmare was the heelwork. At the beginning of the heelwork, I would close the fan and tuck it in the waist of my skirt. After the heelwork, I had just four counts to get it out and open again. Fumbling, it would take me eight. Pio would purse his lips and darken his eyes.

But, by comparison to his depression, his blistering impatience was a blessing.

~

The *Caracoles* started on a fresh note for both Pio and myself. And Julio returned. I walked into Pio's studio one morning and there he was, sitting sloe-eyed and superior, his guitar across his lap. "I thought it over," he said to me, "and decided to accept your apology."

Too confused to ask, "Apology for what?" I began dancing as he began playing. It was the first time I heard the music live by my side. Fast, lilting, it bounced me out of my feet. Moving with sweet ease through Pio's gracious choreography, I forgave Julio his insolence, Pio everything.

And knew I would be eating thistles for lunch.

· 19 ·

VERDE

Pio went from the hopelessness of December to a jubilant January. Whether he leapt out of his depression by himself, or was catapulted out of it by Aurora's crisis, he seemed to be over it. Seemed to be. Pio's moods were like shattered glass; his students had to walk on the shards.

~

Under the Andalucían sun, paint peels in six months; buildings are white-washed twice a year. But the pristine yellow and white world known to tourists was not Pio's *barrio*.

The shabbiest in Sevilla, the *barrio* was fit only for artists and Gypsies. Every building pitted and scraped, dirty paint peeling in blotches. Among the other buildings on Pio's street, his was no different.

He complained to me every day. "Nobody knows who I am, Doloré. Nobody comes in to say, 'Hello. You're Pio Mateo Mendoza, the great flamenco teacher who used to be the great dancer! No. They walk right by my studio without ever seeing it.'"

But one morning mid-January, I turned the corner off Feria onto Matamoros and was jolted by a bright green wall half a block away. Pio's.

Wide-eyed, big mouthed, Pio was out on the sidewalk to meet me. He took me by the elbow and gestured with a quick flick of his nose towards the front of his building. Newly painted.

"*Verde*," he said with a smile, the spaces showing between his back teeth. "*Verde!*"

"Yes. Green," I answered in English, too unsettled to think in Spanish.

"Huh?"

"*Verde*," I replied.

Pio smiled again. "Now everybody will see my studio," he said.

And they would.

"I painted it myself, Doloré!"

And he had. The new paint ended raggedly at the top of the double doors. The wall was a smear of thick and thin brush strokes. And lumps. Pio had painted right over the peeling shreds, carrying them along with his brush. Gouges left by passing cars he had filled with pools of paint.

I stepped around the puddle of green dribbling onto the sidewalk and tried to think of something good to say.

But Pio didn't need my praises; he was well-pleased with himself and didn't want to leave the sidewalk.

I finally eased him inside for my lesson. A fiasco. Ducking in and out of the double doors, he grabbed every passerby to show off his new wall. (He pushed old Tomás, all bones and nearly blind, so close that he got paint on his nose. "I can see it now," Tomás said. "It's green!")

Pio paid no attention to my dancing that morning. Once in a while he yelled, "That's not right!"

"Well," I'd yell back, "then what should I be doing?"

"It doesn't matter," he'd say, and run outside again.

Halfway through my 'lesson,' Pio decided everybody in the corner bar needed to know about his new paint job. And no doubt

Pio needed a beer.

He left the studio. I sighed and sat down next to Joselito.

Joselito had just returned from Barcelona. A housepainter perennially unemployed, he had gone there to work. Now he was back, more willing to cope with no money than leave Sevilla.

I muttered something, "...that god-awful green."

"Oh, *sí*, Doloré," he replied, "it's awful. But if you think the green's bad, well, Pio really wanted purple."

"Purple!" I said. That was the first time I had heard of 'purple.'

"*Sí*, I offered to paint him a nice beige wall. But no. We went all over looking for purple paint and wound up at old Miguel's store near the Alameda. Well, he didn't have it either. But he had bright green. So Pio, he decided on that. Like it was his idea all along. Then Pio asked Miguel for the paint free 'cause Miguel was supposed to know who Pio was. Well, Miguel bellowed 'No!' like a bull and jerked open the front door. Me, he didn't have to tell twice. I left. Pio he had to throw out. And Pio called him a *hijo de puta* from the street. But he admitted he was going to have to pay for the paint."

"So what did you do?"

"We walked, Doloré. All the way to Diego's bar. And Pio held out his hand like a collection plate and Diego gave him what he had on him. Then we walked all the way back to Miguel's."

"I bet old Miguel wasn't happy to see you."

"No, but Pio pulled out the *pesetas* and Miguel didn't say a word. He just went in the back and came out with a box with two big cans in it. Then leave it to Pio to make a big stink about the paint: 'It better be good and it better be bright.' Then he asked Miguel for the brushes—free. Well, Miguel's face turned bright red.

I left quick. Pio, he just strolled out the door with the big box of paint and his nose up in the air. Old Miguel, he slammed the door so hard his windows shook."

Joselito stopped to light a cigarette. I asked him, "So where did Pio finally get the brushes?"

"I gave him some old ones I had, Doloré. Then I went back with him to the studio. Only I had to follow him 'cause he didn't want to be seen on the street with a housepainter."

~

Pio came back from the bar and my lesson resumed—more or less. He kept opening and closing the big double doors, inviting everybody in off the street for a glass of wine and a lengthy "who he was." Even wrapped in woolen tights and extra sweaters, I couldn't keep warm. And in the cold, Julio couldn't play as fast as he usually did. Good. I wasn't dancing very fast.

Chilled to the bone, I left my lesson early. Pio didn't notice. He was moving his photographs around, making room for a big poster of himself as a young dancer, and talking to himself: "Now everybody knows that Pio Mateo Mendoza has an important studio in Sevilla!"

~

That night, Heike, Mariano, and I went looking for flamenco in the small bars.

We had walked all the way across Sevilla before we found flamenco at the Carbonería.

'The Carb' the Americans called it. An old coal yard turned into an outdoor bar, the sooty soil lush with greenery. Patrons sat at tables in waist-high ferns or stood at the bar, drink in hand, feet in foliage. Palm trees sheltered the Carb from the cool of January.

On the far side of the coal yard, we saw Pio in his white suit seated at a long table with some of his nephews from Alcalá. He called us over and we joined him. Of the nephews, I only knew Antonio and Julio. I wasn't introduced to the others; I suspected Pio couldn't remember their names. The nephews were happily flamenco, Antonio rapping rhythms on the table with short sticks.

Pio was glowing. A wall painted green and Pio's vision of himself changed: he was the center of the world again.

Slightly drunk, he stood up to sing. Like sudden sunlight through leaves, he came out of his ego. With his whole soul in his mouth, he sang his affection for his nephews, his praise for Mariano's music, for Heike as *aficionada,* and his hopes for my future. Then an Alegrías:

> What can you give me that I don't
>   already have?
> Well, you can give me the heels,
> The heels to my boots,
> And I will dance for you!

And he did dance. His waistline spreading under his white jacket, it was not the young Pio who had flashed onto the stage like an early storm. But he was still quick, able to snap his turns and bump a hip. And his heelwork could pluck sound even from the soil.

But he didn't dance long.

The manager of the Carb had been standing to one side, arms folded, watching. Before Pio finished, he walked up to him, tapped him on the shoulder, and quietly told Pio to stop.

Pio stopped, "Huh?"

The manager replied, "Noise."

Heike retorted, "You had rock here last night!"

Antonio added, "I'll stop the sticks."

But the manager snapped, "It's over." And to Pio, "Out!"

Pio withered in his white suit; his deflation was like the sun sinking. The rest of us were stunned.

Not Antonio. Angry, he threw the sticks at the manager's feet. (I said, "uh-oh" under my breath.) Bartenders ran over, surrounded him and walked him briskly out of the Carb, Pio and the rest of the nephews behind, Pio shaking his head and saying, "I don't understand."

I didn't understand either, but I started for the front gate. Heike put a hand on my arm. "Don't go out there," she said.

Mariano, Heike, and I sat down at an unobtrusive table.

Sirens. Mariano went out front to see. He came back to tell us Antonio had been arrested, but no one else. We were served drinks as if nothing had happened.

As we left the Carb, I was asking the same questions as Pio, "I don't understand. It seems like all a big mistake."

"The mistake," Mariano replied, "was not that Pio got thrown out. But that someone let him in. He runs up big bills and then he ducks out a side door."

Still, I felt for Pio. It had been his big night. I needn't have worried.

As I came in the studio the next morning, Pio said, "The Carbonería, it's a dump. I'm not going there anymore, Doloré. They don't know who I am."

Pio complained about not being recognized or appreciated but he took no time with being humiliated. No Gypsy does.

But he did take time to be angry. His green wall became a signal: don't try me; don't touch me.

He was no longer inviting passersby into his studio. Instead, he poked his head out the door every two minutes to see if a pedestrian was walking too close to his wall. Or worse—a car was scraping it.

~

That night a car did pass too close.

I was greeted on the sidewalk the next morning by a horror-stricken Pio waving at his wall with a shaking hand. "See. See," he said. "See what they did!"

I couldn't see anything. But Pio put his finger on a white spot the size of a quarter—and moaned.

· 20 ·

EL FENOMENO

Now there was no peace in any of Pio's classes.

The sound of a car or even a bicycle, and Pio was out the studio and down the street. Drivers were losing control at the sight of the little bug-eyed man running after them, waving his arms, loudly cursing them out.

Julio and I gave up; the doors stayed wide open.

My lessons didn't disintegrate completely. Julio continued playing for me, not waiting for Pio's emphatic *"un, do,"* and I continued dancing.

Two days of this and I went to Aurora to complain. What I expected from her, I don't know.

She was sitting up on the sofa again, wearing a new pink chenille bathrobe as big as a bedspread. Pio had bought it for her. Cheap. Every move she made, pink fuzz floated in the air.

"Pio," I started, "he's not paying any attention to his students, not to me, not to anybody, not to—"

But Aurora wasn't listening. "Oh, Doloré," she interrupted, "now 'cause of the new paint everybody knows who Pio is. And it'll be like it used to be before he was in the hospital, when he had lots of students."

Then Aurora, never stopping when she had said enough, added, "Now Pio, he won't be scared anymore."

"Scared?" I asked. But I didn't have to. I always sensed it, a current running in Pio, dark red, long with fear, and connected to his scar.

"*Sí.* 'Cause now Pio's famous again, he won't come back."

"Who won't come back?"

"That old Guardia," she replied, and clamped her mouth shut.

~

Walking to the studio the next morning, my weary experience told me this day would be no different. It wasn't. But Pio's behavior didn't faze Julio. Between smoking, tuning his guitar, and warming his hands, he played and we made the best of the situation. I asked him questions: "In the *silencio*, where does the *cante* come in? What's the music for this step?"

Julio gave no verbal explanations. He responded by playing. Our conversation was two languages that understood each other.

Interspersed with a third, profanity—from Pio, either out in the street or standing at his bar drinking. Pio kept a bottle of whiskey on a lower shelf behind his bar. He venerated that bottle. He had found it one morning, seal unbroken, in a dark doorway and never had opened it. "Doloré, it's only for emergencies," he'd say.

This morning he opened it. He poured himself a jigger and took a sip. Then, hearing a car, he ran out on the street, yelled at the driver, came back in, finished the jigger, poured a new one. And waited for another car.

I was wishing he'd get drunk, forget his damn wall, and remember me. I was dancing in tight flickers of his attention like a strobe light—on, off, on, off.

We were halfway through my 'lesson' when a car with a flat tire pulled up in front. Pio, busy with the whiskey, didn't notice at first. But when he realized a car was next to His Wall, he ran out the

144

front door. Next, Pio's hysterical screams.

Julio in one count was guitar down, fists clenched, and out the door after him. I was stuck to the spot, watching as Pio, face red, voice screeching, was swearing at the driver, who stood with mouth dropped open, a tire iron in his hand.

Julio grabbed Pio by the shoulders, swung him hard around, and shoved him back into the studio, Pio, his eyes like ink wells, yelling, "Nobody's ever going to raise a tire iron to me again!"

He collapsed into a chair, holding his head with both hands, rocking back and forth, Julio saying, "Pio, the guy just has a flat. It's just a flat."

Then Pio started wailing. I wanted to leave the scene alone like a nightmare; I went into the dressing room, sat on the floor, pulled up my knees and put down my head. His wails went right through me.

I waited until it was quiet, changed clothes, and went back into the studio. Pio was still rocking and holding his head, Julio still holding out a whiskey for him.

As I left the studio, the driver was working on his tire. "I didn't touch that crazy little Gypsy," he said, "and he acted like I was killing him. So what's going on?"

I didn't reply; I was too close to crying.

~

I wanted to talk to Joselito, the logical person. He hadn't been in the studio that morning, which meant he was in one of the bars. I found him in the Bar Robles, the third one I tried.

Joselito was seated at a *tertulia*. I took a nearby booth facing him and waited. The men were arguing over the name of a bar where Manuel Torre had sung fifty years before. I nursed a cup of coffee until Joselito broke away and sat down opposite me.

"*Que te pasa*, Doloré?" he asked. What was bothering me? I told him all that had just happened with Pio. Every detail.

"*Aiii...* Doloré," he said, "I could see you were upset when you came in." He shook his head, "*Pobre El Pio*—poor old man. He was *un fenomeno* in his time, but now he's just a poor old man."

"Maybe it's not my business," I said, "but I do care about Pio and I'd like to know what's going on."

"*Sí,* Doloré, but it's nasty."

"That doesn't surprise me."

Joselito lit a cigarette, smoked a bit, finally spoke. "You know, Pio, he couldn't keep his hands off the women. Even the young girls. Especially the young girls. So there was this student of his, maybe fifteen, maybe sixteen, very pretty. Well, Doloré, you can use your imagination."

Knowing that anything I might imagine about Pio would be inadequate, I pressed Joselito, "So, what do you mean? You mean Pio put his hands on the girl?"

"Oh, *sí,* Doloré, in the dressing room, after a lesson, hands all over her. He even pulled up her skirt. Well, she ran home crying. Doloré, her father was a Guardia."

"Oh my God."

"*Sí,* Doloré. That same night, he came after Pio with a tire iron. He almost killed Pio. There was blood all over the street. Pio, when people found him, he was more dead than alive."

Then I did cry.

Joselito ordered me more coffee. I sipped it and said, "Aurora told me Pio's still afraid of the Guardia."

"*Sí.* He's afraid the Guardia's going to come back and finish him."

"But the Guardia must be in prison."

"Maybe in your country, Doloré. But this is Spain, and Pio's a Gypsy."

"You're telling me the Guardia got off?"

"Not really. He and his whole family were moved up north. He's stationed somewhere in Galicia."

"Joselito, I don't call Galicia 'prison.'"

"No, Doloré, but under Franco, he could have killed Pio and still gotten off."

"He damn near did kill Pio. Even with what Pio did, a year in the hospital!"

"*Sí,* a year and lots of operations."

"Joselito, you don't really think that Guardia will come back, do you?"

"No. That's all in Pio's head. That's why it's such a clan secret. Anybody mention the Guardia, or even a tire iron, and Pio, he goes crazy. But Doloré, he's survived. And in another way, he's changed. The hospital, it changed him. If you think he's awful now, you should have known him before. Everybody was beneath him. Me? He wouldn't even speak to me on the street."

"Joselito, he still treats you badly."

"Oh, *sí,* Doloré. I do put up with him. But it's because Pio, he was everything he says he was. Nobody could do the things he did. He was like an insect. Fast. Blink your eyes, Doloré, and he was on the other side of the stage. And someday, Pio, he won't be here anymore."

It had helped to talk to Joselito. But I was wondering what came next. "I can't just go back to the studio tomorrow," I said, "like nothing happened."

"Why not?" he replied. "That's what Pio will do."

~

The next morning, Pio had lost all interest in his green wall. Back teaching in earnest, he took me apart in the *Caracoles*. I was very happy.

But Pio's green wall dragged on the *barrio*. Everybody had an opinion, mostly bad. A few days later, his landlord came by. "It looks like a goddamn whore house," he yelled at Pio. "Paint it over!"

Pio yelled back, "Go to hell! Paint it yourself."

So the landlord sent around two workmen. They painted the wall light beige without priming it. The green bled through in blotches.

Pio had the only camouflaged building in the *barrio*.

· 21 ·

LA LOTERÍA

Pio bought one lottery ticket a week. For all the months I had been in Sevilla, he had won nothing.

Tickets were sold on the street. When Pio heard a vendor, he would run out of the studio, buy a ticket, run back, and tack it to the top of his bar. But when his green wall was under siege, Pio forgot.

Aurora remembered for him. Still recuperating, she was sitting out on her balcony when the vendor came by. She lowered a few coins in a basket and then pulled it back up with her ticket in it.

A few mornings later, her little eight-year-old niece, Luz, was visiting, She saw the numbers on TV, compared them to Aurora's ticket, and told Aurora she had won.

Crying with excitement, Aurora lumbered down the stairs in her bathrobe, ticket in hand, and yelled at a neighbor's car to drive her to the studio. Lise and Joaquin were there. They piled Pio and Aurora into a taxi and went with them to the lottery office in the city hall. Only one hitch: the money had to be transferred from Madrid directly into a bank account. Another taxi to a bank.

Pio was filling out the forms to open an account when Aurora let it slip that it was her ticket that had won. Nothing would do but the account also had to be in her name. But Aurora could only sign her name with an 'X.' Back to the flat to find some proof of who she was, then back to the bank, the whole day spent running between the bank and the flat, Aurora still in her pink chenille bathrobe.

~

Arriving that day for my lesson, the door was locked. No sign of Pio.

When it came to his studio schedule, Pio, very un-Gypsy, was punctual and he was consistent.

Worried that something had happened in Alcalá, I went looking for Joselito for word. I couldn't find him. I called Heike from a bar, no answer. I walked to Pio and Aurora's flat, no one. Then I decided to go home and wait for word to come to me.

Manolo came up to my door about six p.m. "A party," he said, "at the studio." I followed him down to the street. I could hear the party a block away.

Manolo and I arrived at Pio's studio. It was filled to the walls with people and smoke, every flat surface covered with wine glasses and paper plates of fried fish and potatoes.

Julio and Joaquin, drunk enough to get along, were playing together, heads and guitars almost touching. Pio and a woman I didn't know were singing the *Bulerías*. Lise was dancing. As soon as I walked in, she danced over to me and pushed me into the center of the studio. The only *Bulerías* I knew was a short one; I danced the same steps over and over. Spirits high, no one knew the difference.

Finally I got away, grabbed Lise's arm and asked her in English, "What the hell is going on?"

Lise, all smiles, "Oh, don't you know?"

"No, I don't know."

"He won!"

"Who? What?"

"Pio. The lottery."

"My God," I said. "How much?"

"Thirty thousand dollars."

"My God!"

~

No one who knew Pio expected him to do anything sensible with the money. And Pio, except for a happy gurgling in the back of his throat, wasn't telling.

But the gossip at Heike's filled me in.

By Tuesday, every bar in Sevilla knew of Pio's big win at the lottery and they were all courting his business, certainly those he owed money to. But Pio didn't bother himself with the ratty little bars in his *barrio*.

He went instead to the big, posh, expensive bars that catered to affluent Spaniards—the men who spent their days in clubs on Sierpes looking out at the street through one-way glass, spent their nights eating and drinking until three in the morning.

Pio went to these bars, the sparkling bars of the Barrio Santa Cruz, where he wined and dined everyone. A different night, a different bar. One thing, though, remained the same—Pio made sure he was the center of attention.

Not that anyone had illusions about who Pio was. Everyone in Sevilla is catalogued and classified; no one is missed. Pio was known and disliked. First, because he was a Gypsy, and second, because he was obnoxious.

But anyone willing to buy food and drink in Sevilla earns the honor of being listened to.

Pio would go into a bar, nose high, well-dressed (he had his white suit cleaned), rap the counter with his knuckles, and loudly announce, "I am Pio Mateo Mendoza. I was the best flamenco dancer in the world. Now I am the best teacher in the whole world!"

Then he'd raise his glass and buy a round for everyone.

Cheers would go up. The men would mill around the small figure in the white suit shining like a light bulb. A little backslapping, inquiries for his health, that of his woman's, and Pio would be off and running, telling everybody about himself and his career.

As soon as interest began to flag, a touch of boredom set in, he'd quickly order another round of drinks and *tapas* for everybody.

Pio went through $15,000 in fourteen days.

The recognition he had not gotten from his green wall, he bought—and considered it money well spent. Although once the money was gone, no more people were saying his name than before the lottery.

Two weeks and he had nothing to show for his big win.

But Aurora—Pio had admitted, begrudgingly, that half the money was hers—had a lot to show for it.

~

Aurora's first purchase was a big brown leather purse. She couldn't write a check, so she took the money out of the bank in cash. For two weeks she carried around a bankroll in Sevilla, the city with the highest rate of petty street crime in Europe.

Her second purchase was a bedroom set. Aurora, who had grown up sleeping on the ground, who had never known anything in her marriage but cheap furniture, suddenly saw a vision in a furniture store window: an art-deco bedroom set, black lacquer with chrome trim.

She asked me to go with her to the store, "'Cause you're American, Doloré. You know things."

While the middle-aged clerk stood nervously buttoning and unbuttoning his cardigan, Aurora squinted at herself in the chrome trim on the bedstead, the dresser, and the armoire.

She touched the chrome, left a fingerprint, spit on her handkerchief, rubbed it out. She opened every drawer of the dresser. They slid without a sound. She opened the big armoire, looked at the black dustless shelves, the lacquered wood giving back her reflection. She said, "Ooh."

Then to me, "I want it." Then to the clerk, "I want it." Without a word, he handed her the price tag.

Aurora opened her leather bag, took out all the money, and put it in his hands. He counted it out carefully, twice, and put the rest back in Aurora's purse.

But when the set was delivered, Aurora had nothing new to put in the new armoire. So she bought fifty yards of imported Belgian lace to fill the shelves. And for the closet section, she bought herself a full-length fur coat.

Then she settled all her bills with the green grocer, the fish man, the bread man, the butcher, and the woman who sold eggs and butter. She didn't settle one penny on Pio's bar bills.

Next, she told Pio she was going to take Sofia to the Costa Del Sol for a week.

Pio put up a mighty fuss.

Aurora told me all about it. "Pio," she said, "he didn't want me spending any money on Sofia. But I knew that Sofia was getting old. And maybe she's even older than she thinks she is."

~

Sofia guessed her age to be 85. Her hair was a few gray strands, strong as steel, that she wrapped around her head. Her teeth had fallen out years before. She wore a plain brown dress and two wool shawls, even in summer. Fat, she bulged everywhere; the only shoes that fit her feet were men's bedroom slippers.

The oldest woman in her clan, Sofia was in charge of the

women and children. She held occult power in the clan: she could read the future on hands and faces. She also read pebbles, twigs, baby teeth, and goat turds. And she watched the sky for omens: the arc of a rainbow around the sun, one cloud separate from the others, a bird caught in the wind.

Watching and listening, she sat out on the street in front of her house every day in an overstuffed chair. Aurora's father, Esteban, had put homemade rockers on the chair. The littlest children liked to crawl under it and push it hard so Sofía was thrown back and forth.

Sofía would laugh; she could laugh at anything, almost.

But if something made Sofía unhappy, no one on the street of Gypsies sang; the street was sullen and quiet. She could smell anger in the clan, even when it was out of her sight and hearing.

If there was whispering nastiness between the women, she would call them together in a circle around her. Sitting, rocking, she'd scan the sky and say, "Listen. Listen to the winds. They are shaking their rattles. It's a warning, 'cause you're fighting among yourselves. Make it up between you, the winds are saying, or the next baby born—will be born dead!"

Nobody argued with Sofía.

With the children she was gentler. She'd draw circles in the dirt with one big toe sticking out of a slipper while she listened to their prattle. Then she'd tell each one what she knew they needed to hear. Aurora as a little girl needed to be told she was pretty.

Aurora was Sofía's favorite grandchild. When no children were born to Pio and Aurora, Sofía burned special herbs, buried eggs in sand, chanted ancient prayers. Even talked to a doctor who said nothing an old Gypsy woman could understand—except for one thing: Sofía told Pio that maybe it was his fault, and not Aurora's, that they couldn't make babies.

Pio never forgave her.

"Well, Doloré," Aurora went on, "I wanted to give Sofía something. She hadn't been to the beach since she was little. But Pio, he got mad. When I said she might die, Pio said Sofía would never die; she'd always be around to annoy him. So, Doloré, I called Sofía in Alcalá and told her I wanted to take her to the beach with the money from the lottery. Pio didn't want me to spend it. But, Sofía, she said she'd handle Pio. She told him that she would tell everybody it was really him and not me that couldn't make the babies.

"It's not him, Doloré, I know that. But Pio's face, it went all white and he said I could take Sofía anywhere I wanted."

· 22 ·

BULERÍAS

Marbella. White hotels, boats, sails, beaches, people. No dusky-skinned Gypsies wanted.

~

Aurora, wearing her fur coat over a red dress with green polka dots, took a taxi to Alcalá. She picked up Sofía, wearing her bedroom slippers and the same brown sack she always wore.

Arriving at the biggest hotel in Marbella, Sofía's feet had swollen so much in the taxi she couldn't wear even her bedroom slippers. She walked into the hotel barefoot. Her big brown feet splayed out, she left prints on the white carpet.

"There were lots of bells when we came in," Aurora told me later. "And two men at the desk said we couldn't stay 'cause we didn't have reservations."

But Sofía approached Marbella straightforwardly. She told Aurora in *Caló* to just push the money in their faces. Aurora opened her big purse and the money surged forward like sea foam.

Sofía and Aurora were escorted by private elevator to a suite of rooms. "We were way at the top of the hotel, Doloré. We had three rooms, all white, and an all-white bathroom. And there were glass doors out to a big terrace and a little blue swimming pool. Anything we wanted was brought up to us. Just like the man at the desk said, we didn't ever have to go down to the lobby. They sent us a basket of fruit every day and flowers and a newspaper. But we sent that back."

"Sofía and me," Aurora went on, "we ate our breakfast with our feet in the pool. Lunch we ate at the edge of the terrace and watched the boats. Then at night, we ate in bed and watched TV on a big screen."

Nights were also white telephones tucked between ears and chins—long distance calls to family in Barcelona, lengthy calls listening to the gossip, to the babbling of a baby, to the women singing into the receivers.

"It was sunny, Doloré, not like summer, but sunny. Me, I swam in my underwear 'cause I couldn't find a bathing suit my size. Sofía, she just wrapped a sheet around herself and waded." Sofía and Aurora basked in the white world for a week.

Leaving the hotel, Aurora was presented with the bill, a long list, itemized. But Aurora couldn't read numbers any more than she could read words. She set her purse on the desk, took out all the money with both hands and put it in front of the manager. He sorted it into neat bundles, counted it, and handed a few *pesetas* back to her.

Aurora had only enough money left to take Sofía home to Alcalá in a taxi. Then, in her fur coat, she walked from Sofía's house to the bus stop a mile away. She got on the bus to Sevilla, gave the conductor her last few coins, and sat looking out a window.

"Pio," she told me, "he was upset when I got home with no money.

"So I called Sofía to tell her I spent every bit of the money and ask her if that was all right. And she said to me, 'Aurora, here the men are fighting over money. The children are lying for it. The women are jealous 'cause of it. And you ask me is it all right that you spent it? Aurora, I'm proud of you for getting rid of it!'"

~

Two weeks later, Sofía died.

It rained the day she died. Big lines of water slanted across the sky. The women ran outside and collected their children. But Sofía went on rocking and smoking. The rain got harder, then stopped as suddenly as it had started. The women and children came out of the houses. Sofía was still in her chair, soaking wet, head back, her unseeing eyes staring straight up at the sky. She was smiling.

Gypsy death does not often end in a cemetery. Burials can be in illegal places—along a river, in a cave, an unmarked grave in a forest. But Sofía's clan was urbanized; she had a funeral and was buried in the cemetery in Alcalá.

Aurora was very distressed over Sofía's death. Pio was not. He returned to Sevilla right after the funeral. He announced to me my first lesson back that we were going to start *Bulerías*.

~

For the Gypsies, the *Bulerías*, by noontime or moonlight, is their cakewalk. After the pain of the *cante jondo* is spent, the lost loves, the salted wounds, it is time for the pithy comments, or ribald nonsense.

The *cante* can be satirical:

> My mother-in-law says nothing;
> She is one of those women
> Who bites with her mouth shut.

It can treat of the heart's misery:

> It is a punishment not to see you,
> It is a torment if I do see you.
> I no longer know which one I want.

Or it can be raucous:

> You threw a lemon at me
> And hit me on the head.
> That's what love can do to you.

A Gypsy *juerga* can begin with *Bulerías,* end with *Bulerías.* And sometimes *Bulerías* is all there is. Its *compás*, strident, swift, hypnotic, is horses' hooves in the bloodstream.

Dancing it, there is no time to think; think and you're done.

At a *juerga,* everyone dances the *Bulerías*, from the shy, skinny children with eyes on the ground, to the grandmas who kick off their shoes and flag their skirts like old *putas.*

The men dance it straight as sticks, knees poking through their pants, elbows through sleeves. Their feet churn the dirt. Twisting and swiveling, the men turn in one spot like spirals of dust.

The women dance round, soft; the women's edges blur. They lean back from the waist rolling the pelvis, arms revolving overhead in slow circles while fingers snap the *compás* and feet shuffle the heelwork.

Couples dance like mating birds dipping and swooping into each other's curves, eyes on the secret spaces between them.

~

I was pleased to start learning the *Bulerías.* I had only a few stale steps, leftovers from California.

Pio developed his choreography in sections. Not bothering how they linked up, he'd switch the sections around; yesterday's first step was not necessarily today's.

Julio had no patience with my learning process. My asking him to slow down for me, or repeat, exactly, what he had just played, was met with a blank stare.

Pio's *Bulerías* was full of swift manueverings of weight and balance. I'd suddenly find myself on the wrong foot to begin a new section. Then he'd scream and I'd have to unwind the steps clear back to the beginning, changing the feet so I would come out with the correct foot to start a new section.

But Julio got his cool withered. Pio, in a new mood, blistered him for not supporting me. While I stood by and smirked.

~

Pio's heelwork for the *Bulerías* was more demanding than ever. After every lesson I'd stagger out of his studio, holding onto the building until my legs stopped shaking.

He encouraged me to find freedom in the solid feel of fast, accurate heels.

Nowhere in California, with no one, was I able to accomplish the level of heelwork I did with him. Some teachers said, "It's all in the thigh muscles." Others said, "It's all in the mind." Pio said nothing. He knew intuitively what exercises, and how much repetition, I needed.

From the very beginning, he understood me a great deal better than I understood him.

In his studio, my body found the Gypsy line, its downward plunge. *Compás* slipped into me and became my own. These things happened mysteriously; I did not know when or how.

But Pio knew. Back in September he had said, "By April, Doloré, you will be dancing like a Gypsy. And the heelwork, it'll be easy for you."

I hadn't believed Pio in September. In April, however, mind and muscle came together. The heelwork became a clear path, no ominous beasts of uncertainty blocked my way. I could speed up, slow down, take my ease, in even the most complicated steps.

A great deal is made of heelwork in flamenco. The purists

shudder, and I shudder with them, at the loss of meaning and *gracia* in flamenco.

But for the time being, I reveled in the heelwork for the *Bulerías*, a sizzle of electricity.

Absorbed, happy, I wasn't ready when Pio announced the studio was closing for a week. "Again!" I yelled.

"*Sí*, Doloré. It's the Holy Week."

"But you just reopened!"

"*Si*, Doloré. But everything closes for Semana Santa."

Pio's announcement came as a shock. Not only because I would lose more studio time, but because the end was so clearly in sight.

It was mid-April. Then came May, June, and I would be leaving Spain.

SEMANA SANTA

Barmen in Sevilla tally up drinks in chalk in front of a customer, then wipe the marks away with a soft white cloth.

One of the oldest bars has deep wells worn in the wood. I used to put my fingers in the bottom of the wells just so I could touch Sevilla a hundred years ago.

But a hundred years is nothing to Sevilla. It took four hundred years to build its cathedral; the ritual of Semana Santa is five hundred years old.

Night and day, from Palm Sunday to Easter, the sound of drums and trumpets ricochets through the narrow streets and bounces off the buildings.

Christ is proclaimed. He has come again. But not on two feet.

The thin polychromed figure stretched on a plain wooden cross seems to move by itself.

The huge wooden float, called a *paso,* is carried by fifty men hidden beneath velvet draperies, their backs bending like cresting waves, feet shuffling on hot concrete for twelve hours at a stretch.

In a slow rolling dance, the Christ figure sways gently over the crowds rushing at it in ecstatic belief. The wooden image has turned to flesh and bone. Divine Life is coming up the street.

~

It would have been easy for me, and safe, to watch the Holy

Week processions from my rooftop; it overlooked a main parade route. But I had to be on the streets, the shivers running up and down my spine.

The streets in Spain are always empty. Even full, they are empty. Except at Semana Santa. Then they are crowds who have left their reason.

Wrapped in bodies, near to frightened, I learned to watch for openings, skirt in and out of the edges of the mobs pushing towards the rocking crosses.

All week the *pasos* pressed on, one after another, through the streets. *Pasos* of the Christ, of the Via Dolorosa, of Golgotha, of the Descent from the Cross.

Even more of the Virgin.

A Papal bull, a 'now hear this' from the Vatican, was read from the pulpits reminding Sevilla that Jesus is the primary focus of Christian worship.

But the Sevillanos remained Marianists: it is the Virgin they most adore. "Beautiful!" the crowds called out to her, "Beloved!" "Darling sweetheart!"

The favorite is the Macarena, the Virgin of the Gypsies.

Riding under a canopy of gold lace and long tassels that swing to the beat of drums, her eyes cry real pearls for her Child struck to the cross. Her delicately carved wooden hands, stretched out to the people seeking her, are blood-spattered.

Around her dusky face, the color of an Arabian pony, she wears a halo of white lace. Three hundred white candles at her feet throw a shower of lights on her gold brocade cape. Her enormous crown shoots sixteen gold stars and a diamond cross.

She is accompanied by trumpets, by a fife and drum band, by clergy, by Guardia Civil in dress uniforms. And by barefoot *penitentes* peering through the peep holes in pointed hoods rising three feet.

Lit by sunlight, the *penitentes* are not fearsome.

But by night, the smoke of candles and incense ascends past the strained features of the Christ figures, past the tear-stained faces of the Virgins. It hovers over the dimly lit crowds pressing for air in the tight streets.

Then the black and purple hoods of the *penitentes* rise wicked, evoking other trees, bodies swaying by fire-light.

I would want to slink into doorways. Yet a moment later, I'd be carried along by people running to greet the next *paso* coming up the street.

~

Sevilla is criticized for lack of solemnity during Semana Santa.

Ronda maintains a week of holy silence. Madrid is ominous, medieval, chains clanking on ankles, bloody footprints on the street.

But the Sevillanos extend a joyous welcome to the Christ and to the Virgin.

High-pitched songs, arrows of love, *Saetas* they are called, are sung to the *pasos* from the balconies. All Sevilla listens while the men carrying the *pasos* kneel like resting camels.

> Look at Him coming.
> Jesús, the All-powerful!
> At each step
> Lilies and carnations
> Blossom beneath His feet.

and

> Oh Virgin of Hope,
> Oh Mother of Forgiveness,
> The sun dresses in finery

To see you pass;
The moon showers you
With its white light.

Flamencos like Joaquin, hired by the religious brotherhoods, sing *Saetas* to the *pasos*. The *Saetas* are rarely sung spontaneously as they once were. But the floating sound, seemingly sourceless, nevertheless drives silken nails into the heart.

~

Semana Santa ended abruptly on Easter Sunday. Mass was celebrated in the cathedral in the morning. A bullfight, the other religion of Sevilla, was fought in the afternoon.

I didn't attend the *corrida*. By April, I was drained of bullfighting. I had tasted it, and it remains with me.

As for Pio, his religious attitudes were ambivalent: he spent Semana Santa in a bar. But he regularly lit votive candles, and he always crossed himself when he saw purple. His attitude toward clergymen was, like all Spaniards, cynical. Toward nuns, however, he had an awesome fear mixed with earthy humor.

A couple of days after Semana Santa, while the candle wax was still being cleaned off the streets, I was back in the studio, glad to see Pio.

He met me smiling at the door, handed me a glass of red wine and sat down and talked to me. Conversation with Pio was a rarity. I often felt that I was only a number: I took a ticket and when my number came up, he started teaching.

But this morning, it was "Doloré, *mi alma*," some wine shared, and Pio pleasant and amiable. I should have been forewarned.

"You won't believe it, Doloré," he said, "but a nun, short and fat in a long habit, came in one morning and asked me if I taught the

Bulerías."

Sipping my wine, I interjected, "Pio, a nun?"

"*Sí*, Doloré. And I was thinking—how was I going to teach her in that habit. I mean, would she lift her skirts? I was afraid she would. Then she asked me about tuition, Doloré. And when I told her, she said didn't I have special rates for a religious."

"So what did you tell her?"

"Well, I answered her real carefully. 'Cause you know, Doloré, the nuns, they're not real. I mean, when I walk by the convent and the door is open, and it's always open, you never see any nuns inside. No. So I think the nuns are real when they're outside the convent. But inside, they disappear. They don't have bodies anymore and they can go through cracks. But anyway, Doloré, I was afraid if I gave her a rate she'd become my student. But if I didn't, I'd fry in Hell. So what could I do? I said I'd give her a rate. Then she said 'When?' for the lessons. I said mornings. Then she said her niece was in school. 'Niece? Who? What niece?' I asked. And she said, 'My niece. She's in school in the mornings.'"

"Pio, you mean the lessons weren't for her?"

"No. And that's just what I said, 'You mean the lessons are not for you!' And she lowered her eyes and said, 'Did you think they were?' Then she blushed and wagged her fat hips. Doloré, she was flirting with me! But still that was better than teaching *Bulerías* to those legs under those skirts."

Pio poured me another glass of red wine. We laughed together over the little nun. "But you, Doloré," he said, "that's different. I am proud to teach you my *Bulerías*. And *Feria* is coming!"

Easy, relaxed, off guard, I didn't see what else was coming.

"*Sí*," Pio went on, "and I'm going to rent a *caseta*."

The *casetas* are the small houses, or pavilions, that line the streets of the fairgrounds. The Spaniards use them to entertain. But for the Gypsies, a *caseta* becomes a setting for flamenco, a *Salón de Fiesta*.

"*Sí*, Doloré," Pio went on, "I want a *caseta*, but to rent one, you understand, costs money."

There it was, the wine, the camaraderie, the flattery, all aimed at one thing—money. Mine.

"So, Doloré," Pio said, "I need an advance until June."

"June! Pio, that's outrageous. I've already advanced you to May and now you want more. I'm very sorry but—"

"Then no *caseta*, Doloré, 'cause they cost to rent. And you have to know people. I got lucky 'cause I met this man at City Hall but I have to pay him. Besides, Doloré, it's for you. I want you to dance at the fair. But we have to have a *caseta*."

"What do you mean 'we'? Who's 'we'?" I wanted to know.

"Joaquin, he said he'd come and sing. And Julio will play. So will Mariano. And Lise will dance. Doloré, you will dance. And I will have a company, Los Flamencos de Feria. The best in Sevilla! All the Spaniards will come to the *caseta* of Pio Mateo Mendoza. And they will pay for the privilege."

Pio kept talking but my mind was elsewhere. The chance, most likely my last, to spend a whole week with the Gypsies, to dance with Lise, Joaquin, Mariano, overcame any common sense I had about money.

"And you can dance the *Siguiriyas* and the *Caracoles* and the *Bulerías*." Pio went on. "But we have to rent a *caseta*."

"*Sí*, Pio," I agreed, "we have to rent a *caseta*."

· 24 ·

FERIA DE ABRIL

Reactionary in its reasoning, maddening in its inefficiency, Sevilla is always finding its way backward. It is a city enclosed by a fifteenth century wall that could be easily climbed over—but isn't.

I adapted to Sevilla on its terms, took my crumbs, and structured myself to the measure of its thinking.

Serious endeavors are not Sevilla. The tendrils of the wrought iron street lamps beautify the night, but the bulbs emit only a faint glow. The fountains cool the plazas, but they leak in puddles.

Sevilla achieves its greatness at play. Especially at play.

Sevilla is more itself during the April Fair, *Feria*, than any other time of the year.

~

Small boats wander the Guadalquivir's width without touching either side. In fall, the river's waters are *de aceite antiguo*, the color of aged olive oil. In winter, dim blue, as if washed too often. In April, bright green.

Sunlight and the palm trees along the quay catch the glint of gold, memorial to the river's history. Evenings, the sweet odor of the horses pulling carriages across the Isabel Bridge mixes with cooler air.

The Guadalquivir divides Sevilla in two. Sevilla is on one side of the river, Triana on the other. Triana, "only a *barrio*" to the Sevillanos, considers itself a separate city. Trianeros say their flamenco is more plentiful and more authentic than Sevilla's. But I was never convinced. Triana's fame is its fairgrounds: a miniature city laid out in a grid of streets, used only once a year—for *Feria*.

From all over Europe, exhibits, rides, food concessions, and horse shows converge on the fairgrounds. By night, a city of lights; by day, a thousand dots of color—all moving. Mariano warned me, "See everything, Doloré, and you will miss a lot."

~

After the long processions of bleeding feet and weeping Virgins, the April fair is a huge kiss.

The fair began in the nineteenth century with horse trading. It is still horses. Daily at noon, the finest horses of Andalucía are paraded through the main thoroughfare: chestnuts, dappled grays, pure whites, Arabian ambers, bedecked and festooned with bells and tassels, ribbons and ball fringe.

No one rides like the Spanish ride. It is a gathering of minds, rider and mount moving together as smoothly as a dancer's best day. The men are in formal riding dress, the women in long skirts riding sidesaddle or seated behind the men on pillions. Their long dresses—polka-dotted fantasies in bright whites, reds, purples, pinks, and yellows—drape down over the flanks of the horses.

The *Feria* dresses are an event in themselves. In the horse-drawn carriages the dresses crush together like spring blossoms. In the streets, the dresses billow; tides of cloth rise and fall as the women dance the *Sevillanas*, their hips swinging to the voice of shawl fringe.

Lining the main parade route like brightly painted toy boxes are the *casetas*. Open to the street, each is a small world of sherry, manzanilla tea, and *tapas*. A civility in the fair, a place to entertain friends and family, to sit in white wicker chairs in the shade of red and white striped curtains, to offer a glass of sherry to any horseman that rides up.

But the Gypsy *casetas* are on a narrow, not clean, back street, avoided by horsemen.

Aurora, grieving for Sofía, didn't come to the fair, didn't have her fifty yards of Belgian lace made into a *feria* dress.

But Pio had his *caseta.*

Tiny and cheap, furnished with clanking folding chairs, card tables that wobbled, and bare bulbs hanging from the ceiling, he dressed for it as if it were the Opera House. He had bought, on credit of course, a new *traje de jinete*—a gray cropped jacket, white shirt with lace cuffs, black and gray striped trousers, gray felt cordobés. Although he had no horse, he carried a black crop.

He stood at the entrance to his *caseta,* his chin and his nose up, and waited to greet the Spaniards. Thinking his elegant dress and the big splurge he had made with the lottery money would attract them, he found out differently. They did not flock to his shabby little *caseta*, his *Salón de Fiesta*, as he expected. He was left with only the Gypsies coming in and out to sing and dance for each other. As far as I was concerned, that was the better part.

But Pio was not satisfied. He decided if the Spaniards wouldn't come to him, he would go to them. He spent most the week crashing their *casetas*. At night, the Spaniards had their big parties. The *Sevillanas* was danced until dawn; there was no end of music, food, and wine. A small Gypsy, well-dressed, was tolerated.

With Pio gone, his *caseta* became the gathering place for the Gypsies from the neighboring *casetas*. Gypsies I had never met before showed up with food and wine. They sat together singing or danced inside or outside in the street. The Gypsies can dance on rocks or sing to walls. Make a stage on boxes or in the space between two chairs. Pio once said, "Doloré, I can make any step as big as the Opera House or as small as my father's living room."

The old flamencos showed up, dancers and singers in their seventies and eighties, still performing. *'Los Ultimos'* they are called, 'The Best Ones,' fat old ladies, their faces deep ruts in the road, and the men with their bellies hanging over their belts.

There was Tía Ana, so fat she had to be helped in and out of her chair. She danced and sang, cackling like a rooster between soft, toothless gums. Her legs, tree trunks in baggy stockings, barely moved while she yanked her skirts up and down, bumped her big hips, and told little obscenities with her hands. Her dance sexual, not suggestive—old Gypsies never 'suggest' anything—she had an energy and a spirit that sparked the night.

Tío Tito, jowls like a bull, sat and banged his stick as he pulled the *cante jondo* through his warped throat. His cracked sobs were all that was left of his voice.

But he was more powerful by what he didn't sing than by what he did. *'Era casi na,'* the saying goes, 'His song was almost nothing,' the highest compliment in flamenco. Like a drawing by Matisse done with only one line.

Tía Maria sat on the edge of her chair while she sang, her belly planted on her thighs. She had a spiked nose, cheekbones like cliffs, and a big white rose perched in the middle of her head. Serious, stern, her hard voice spanked the air. She sang straight out what had happened in her life. She had the *duende* of having been where the pain was.

Inside or outside, *Bulerías* was all that was danced, the women in black, big all over, moving like fire. The men flipping their bellies from side to side.

Only in the early morning hours did the dancing stop and the *cante jondo* begin. The Gypsies sobbed, and the sound slid down the necks of the guitars.

~

The Gypsies sped out of my control; I couldn't keep up with them. So I took time out in Mariano's *caseta*. Well-furnished, comfortable, it was on the main street among the Spaniards'. But he expected no Spaniards.

"*Sí*, Doloré," he explained, "the Spaniards will have a reception for me after a concert, but they won't shake my hand."

"Why not?" I asked.

"Because I'm half-Gypsy, Doloré. That's why not."

Heike was at Mariano's *caseta*. She wouldn't go near Pio's, but she did ask me what "the little runt" was up to.

"Pio?" I replied, "He's going around to all the *casetas,* trying to get bookings for his company."

"Don't hold your breath. And you, Doloré, what are you up to?"

"Me? I'm trying to forget I will be leaving."

~

I drank too much at *Feria*. It was almost May, and soon I would have to say my goodbyes to Heike, Lise, Joaquin—people I might never see again. I would have to close the door on Pio, my feelings about him unresolved. See Aurora, sad and grieving, for the last time.

But it wasn't only May I wanted to forget.

Age. It was coming at me like a lesson. I turned fifty-six during Feria. It would have been a perfect place for a birthday party, but I kept it quiet; I was already thinking stateside, where a dancer's age is not only a factor but often the *first* consideration.

But in Spain, I no longer had to concern myself with age.

Spain exposes all sides of life: babies are born in full view on TV, old men piss off bridges, the deformed are seen in broad daylight. As for age, it is all right to live longer. The closer one gets to dying, the more it is assumed one knows.

The *'Ultimos'* had the truth. Their aging bodies, reflecting all they had lived, served to amplify their art.

So why a whole year to develop my own truth and then no place to take it? I leveled the question at Joaquin. His response, "Well, at least, Doloré, you got here. I will never get to the States," didn't resolve my dilemma.

Perhaps Joaquin's response was the right one. I had gotten to Spain. Maybe that was all there was. But it was not something I could accept.

In California, however, there was one person I could dance with who wouldn't measure my art by my age—Rosario.

I wasn't sure I could accept that either.

⋅ 25 ⋅

CUADRO

I thought Pio had forgotten his flamenco company; it was already late in the *feria* week. But Pio hadn't forgotten. He had been going to the Spaniards' *casetas* with a purpose. Then one night, he stood in the entrance to his own *caseta*, riding crop under his arm, and announced that Los Flamencos de Feria would be making its debut "at the biggest *caseta* in the fair!"

"And these Spaniards," he added, "they're related to the Duchess of Alba." I guessed it would be news to the Duchess.

Pio called a rehearsal for the next day at four p.m.; the performance to be at eleven.

The *cuadro*: Joaquin would sing; Julio play; Lise, myself, and Kimiko, the Japanese girl, dance. And Pio would do the *palmas*. A small company but a good one.

Lise, Kimiko, and I had twenty-four hours to come up with two costumes each. Lise had hers stuffed into a duffle bag. She pulled out two for herself, one for me. A massive ironing job. I splurged on a new black leotard to wear with my black practice skirt and a long, red *montoncillo*, the fringe covering the belt line. I bought big red plastic earrings, a flower for my hair, and cajoled the shoemaker into re-dying my red shoes. He said they were past it.

Kimiko found a white dress with blue polka dots at the used store. But she was also dancing the *Farruca*, a man's dance. She needed a frilly shirt and tight pants. Pio sold her his old costume.

But she was a head taller than he was, and long-legged. Kimiko was piecing and patching the costume all through the rehearsal. Ten minutes before the performance, Lise and I sewed her into the pants.

~

The rehearsal was a sketchy "Let's see... What if...?" At 10:30 p.m., we walked over to the *caseta*.

Pio's "biggest *caseta* in the fair" was everything he said it was—cavernous. It made the audience, a respectable Spanish family of thirty people, look insignificant and the hastily built platform, tiny.

We mounted the steps to the platform, sat down in the noisy folding chairs. Squashed together, legs rubbing, I feared for the costumes getting crushed. And even the raised platform didn't give us any distance from the staring faces in the front row. Unnerving.

We opened with the *Sevillanas*, a good warm-up. Versatile as an omelet, it can be danced by couples, by singles, by threes, fours, with castanets, without castanets, with fans, without.

For the first few bars, the *Sevillanas* was a blur; I didn't know if I was performing or rehearsing. I relied on my body to remember the steps before I did. Worse, the *caseta* had an echo. And the platform bounced under my heels.

Sitting back down, I watched anxiously as Julio's chair skittered precariously close to the back edge of the platform. I worried about Joaquin's voice, hoarse at rehearsal, and Lise's left ankle, hurting and weak.

I was feeling no unity with the group; I wasn't the only one.

Cuadro is intimate: the jitters are passed around. Too many nerves, and tempos speed out of control. Too few, and the *cuadro* is sluggish.

But Pio was at his professional best. It was the drumming of his *palmas*, as if there were multiple hands, that pulled us together. Seated in a semi-circle, just 'us,' we faced each other and the audience at the same time. We began to weave the music. Excitement happened; flamenco happened.

Joaquin, who had gurgled the sound at rehearsal, sang like a bird. How did he do what I never felt before? Julio played with more enthusiasm and energy than I had heard in the studio. Kimiko, *la japonesa*, her skin sleek, her nose high-bridged, her line cut from a woodblock, moved through the *Farruca* heelwork, feet pounding like pistons.

Lise's dancing was quicksilver. Hands crossed in front of her face, eyes down, she was *lo gitano*, the most Gypsy.

Siguiriyas, Caracoles, Bulerías were my dances. Above all, *Siguiriyas*. Remembering the time I danced it for Pio's family from Barcelona, I burned to return to the intensity of that morning.

Joaquin sang the opening *letra*:

> *Aiii...*
> Ring the bells.
> Ring them slowly,
> For my love has died
> And my heart.

I ran to the center of the stage on the first *Aiii...* and stood in a long, lunging pose, waiting for him to finish the *letra*. Arms overhead, balanced on the balls of my feet, my legs were shaking with nervousness.

As soon as I was able to move, my fear left me. But the message didn't get to my legs all at once; they felt like they were going to slip out from under me.

Luckily, the first heelwork comes early in the *Siguiriyas*. Retreating to center upstage, I became a cat presence listening to the guitar and readying myself. Then, slamming my heels into the floor, I forced strength up into my legs and my spine.

My confidence returned. Attaching myself to the beat that seemed to go on by itself—some rhythms are not created; they exist—I danced the difficult spiral turns and figure eights of Pio's *Siguiriyas.*

But there were the quiet times when I could stand still, softly padding the *compás* with one foot, then another. Moments when I could be my dreams, be the Gypsy night, become the other.

Pio's *Siguiriyas* is repetitious and long. I danced it that way; I wouldn't shorten a poem; I wouldn't shorten his choreography.

Dancing for the Spaniards, I was hoping for that guttural rush of sound heard at the *festivales,* a roar of approval that begins low, grows louder and louder. It is uniquely Spanish and the nicest thing an audience can do for a flamenco.

It happened for me. Even one old *Doña,* seated right in the middle of the audience, who hadn't looked up more than once from her crocheting, joined in.

I finished the performance knowing I was accomplished. The *sabor,* the essence of flamenco, was me. I didn't wonder who I was in any dance. In the *Siguiriyas,* I was mythic Spain; in *Caracoles,* the white doves of Madrid, wings beating like fans. *Bulerías* I danced as precisely as cut glass with the down-in-the-dirt style of the Gypsies.

Afterwards, back in Pio's *caseta,* he said, "Doloré, you're not a student anymore." Nothing else. But it made me wish fervently for another performance. It wouldn't happen; I knew that. The Gypsies come together quickly—and separate just as quickly.

And, although the performance had gone well, it had its flaws. I wanted to try again, work out the hitches and the quirky transitions that we laughed over back in the *caseta*.

One thing, however, we weren't laughing over—money.

Pio had been paid well for the performance. He bragged about it. And, of course, felt justified in keeping all of it for himself. Wasn't he the one who had made the contact, saw to it that a platform was constructed just for us, publicized the event? Therefore....

By two a.m., the argument over money was well-heated. Julio, Joaquin, and Pio started arguing in *Caló*. Lise and I both wanted to keep out of it. I didn't want to sour my last days in Sevilla, and Lise said she could never win with Pio anyway. So we slipped across the street for something to eat.

By 2:30 a.m., the Gypsies in the nearby *casetas* had gotten into it. It was becoming a street fight. Three a.m., the police arrived. Everyone scattered. Lise and I casually finished our food and went home. *Feria* was over.

~

Sevilla cannot let go of Spring.

The sun pours lilies on the ground and May arrives in white covered wagons, trimmed with lace and pink carnations, parading through the streets on their way westward to the sacred shrine of *La Virgin del Rocío,* Our Lady of the Dew.

The wagons converge on Sevilla from all over Spain, then cross the mouth of the Guadalquivir River by ferry, and then they progress slowly through the Coto Donaña sand dunes to the town of Rocío. Frequent stops for paella cooked over open fires and constant stops for flamenco and wine alleviate the hardships of the pilgrimage.

Pio encouraged me to go on *Rocío*, although every time I asked him what it was like, he would only curl up his nose and say,

"Dusty, Doloré, very dusty."

For Pio, who never liked beaches anyway, the clouds of sand would be intolerable. But Pio really didn't need to leave Sevilla. *Rocío* week was celebrated citywide and around the clock. He kept his studio open. It got so crowded with men coming in off the street for free wine, I had to fight for dance space. Still, I decided to get in as much studio time as I could. The first week of June, I would be leaving Sevilla.

· 26 ·

VAYA CON DIOS

It was during *Rocío* week that I started crying. Someone on the street shouts *"Viva España!"* and the *gente* shout back, *"Qué Viva! Qué Viva!"* That touched me. The Maestranza horse show, lines of white Arabians leaping; I watched them through a blur of tears. Two men, as old as Spain, wrapped in black capes, wearing black *cordobés*, brims touching, sit in a café talking the bullfights. They moved me. Early mornings, the first light on the streets of Sevilla changes the buildings from gray to gold. In the bar, I cried over my hot chocolate and madeleines.

The big things, however—leaving my friends, finishing my studies with Pio, leaving my apartment—these things I didn't cry about. I couldn't admit it was really over.

I was dry-eyed and cool. But night after night, I was having a recurring dream: my suitcase opened to spill paper cutouts, flat as leaves blown from a tree, of Heike, Mariano, Joaquin, Lise, Aurora, and Pio.

By day, I went around my apartment patting its walls. For a year I had practiced in it, thrashed out my problems there, worried over Aurora. Despaired over Pio.

A young German actress would be taking the apartment. She came up with Mack one morning to look at it and complained about everything: a musty smell in the closet, touches of rust on the bathtub, the small rug in the hallway (that I used to practiced on), it was frayed, it was old, it was soiled. On the terrace, she complained there was a tear in the *toldo*. I always enjoyed that slice of light, thin as a knife blade, coming through the tear. She even complained about the view: the church roof had enough dirt to grow a fig tree; there were bats living in the stork's nest. What could be done about that?

I didn't want to turn my apartment over to her. She would add nothing to my memory of it. And this was my fear: my memories would become nothing more than the two-dimensional figures spilling out of my suitcase.

~

The very first day of June, Pio met me outside on the sidewalk, as excited and pop-eyed as when he had shown me his green wall. But he hadn't painted his wall again. Whatever awaited me, awaited inside. He took me by the elbow and pushed me into the studio.

There it was, in the middle of the floor, a free-standing mirror taller than Pio and nearly filling the dance space.

I stood dumbfounded, and chagrined. All year long I had struggled to see myself in the glass of the photographs on his wall. I had pleaded, I had argued. But Pio wouldn't get a mirror. Now here it was, and I was leaving.

"It's a mirror, Doloré," he said.

"I can see that," I replied, "but what's it doing in the middle of the floor?"

"It's not for this studio, Doloré. I'm getting a new studio! Big, big enough for mirrors, and it's on my street and it doesn't cost any more than this one. And I'm going to have a new sign out front!"

(Pio's old tile sign:

LA ACADEMIA

DE BAILES FLAMENCOS

MAESTRO PIO MATEO MENDOZA

SEVILLA, ESPAÑA

had a crack through the middle of his name and hung crooked outside the double doors. Every time he passed it, he'd straighten it with two fingers but it always swung back on a slant.)

Julio and I pushed the mirror up against a wall. For the first time in a year, I saw myself dancing. I said hello to my image, thought my skirt was too long, didn't like my arms, I needed to keep my feet closer together, and so on.

But, no surprise, Pio stopped the lesson short and insisted on walking me the five blocks to his street, pushing my elbow all the way. We turned right onto Espíritu Santo and into the foyer of a building as dark and as fish-smelling as his own. I was back at the beginning. I had come full circle; Aurora would come down a staircase.

She didn't. Instead, Pio and I went down a flight. It was pitch black; I had to hold onto the walls. "Pio," I said, "you've got to put a light over these stairs."

"*Sí*," he responded, "if they need it."

At the bottom, he fumbled for a key, opened a door and flicked on fluorescent lights—another full-circle. His new 'studio' was a storage room filled to the ceiling with broken tables, over-stuffed chairs, ragged sofas, rusty iron bedsteads.

But the room was big, I gave Pio that, more than twice the size of his current studio. "And, Doloré," he said, waving at the mess, "once it's all cleared out, the mirror will be there. Here will be a bar. And chairs all the way around. Lise said she will make me new curtains."

"Curtains? Pio, for what? There're no windows."

"For around the mirror, Doloré, and around a big picture of me on the wall. *Sí*, Doloré," he added, "everybody will know Pio Mateo Mendoza has an important studio in Sevilla!"

Suddenly I envied all the students who would still come to Pio, a great talent in dirty socks. They would put up with his ego, struggle with his money-grubbing, his moods. But they would go away, as I was, with far more than they came with.

I was happy to see Pio off and running, all hope and expectation over his new studio. How else could I leave him?

Then he said to me, "And I will have my *Salón de Fiesta* in this studio, Doloré, and my company. And if you stay—"

"Pio, I'm not going to stay," I heard myself saying.

~

I had already started my goodbyes. First Heike. We were in her dilapidated little Citroen, Heike driving like a shock. Her freckles were small red warning signals. "You," she said, "you people. You come here to study and have a good time—"

I interrupted, put a present for her on the dash, a toilet roll figure of a *caballero* in full *traje de jinete*. She didn't acknowledge it.

Crossing over the river into Triana, we passed the statue of Belmonte, the bandy-legged little bullfighter with the jutting jaw. "And you're here for a few months or a year—"

We passed the old Gypsy quarter, empty, one street named for the Inquisition, "—then you leave." We passed the ceramics factory, the tiles gleaming like stained glass in a dark church, "—and I never see you again!"

Heike had to be salty. It made it so much easier for us to

part.

We parked in a narrow alley and went into Mariano's studio.

He was finishing a lesson; he and a student, heads together, guitars almost touching, were playing a *Guajiras*. His studio was pervasively clean, the walls and floor all wood, all glowing with the same patina as the guitars. I sighed; it was so different from my small dirty place of worship.

Mariano invited Heike and me to a nearby bar for a final drink. A teetotaler, he ordered orange drinks all around. The bottles were sticky but their color sang in the half light of the bar.

"So, Doloré," he said, "we'll meet in New York soon, you and I." We both knew I wouldn't be in New York. But I nodded in agreement; I could pretend. It was easier than admitting I might never see him again. I might never again hear his music live by my side.

He stayed only a few minutes and went back to this studio. Heike and I pushed away the orange drinks and ordered wine. Over our glasses and out a window, we silently watched a group of teenagers dancing the *Sevillanas* on the corner.

It was a different Heike I was sitting with. Her freckles were morning lights. Always around Mariano, her rude, crude face became an apple caught in sunlight. I had seen from the first night in her house that wherever he was, Heike wanted to be. She held onto nothing; the flow of the river was her teacher. With one exception—Mariano.

Heike spoke first. "Mariano," she said, "his loneliness is here in Spain. New York, that's where he wants to be." Her freckles fading, she added, "where his wife and daughter are."

Then abruptly changing the subject, "So, Doloré. Have you seen Aurora? Have you told her you're going?"

"No," I replied, "and I'm not looking forward to it."

~

Aurora, tied to the loss of Sofía, was closed up. Seated by her side on her naugahyde sofa, it felt for a moment like it was in the beginning, when there had been nothing between us, and I thought nothing of her. But again, her sweetness drew me in; I missed her at once. I had learned that the woman who seemed to have no mind at all was altogether *someone*. I held her hand as I told her I was leaving. I wanted to cry; I wanted her to cry. But she took me no further than the surface. I left the flat hurt; I had expected more from her.

~

For a goodbye meal, Lise and Joaquin had invited me to their apartment. Joaquin cooked fish, small like smelts and very tasty. We ate in the shed that was the dining room. Half-way through the meal, Joaquin left us. He said he had a bad hangover, had to go to bed. But Lise said it was because he couldn't stand goodbyes. So the meal ended with just Lise and me telling each other all the ways we would stay connected. I was wearing a silver Mexican bracelet she had admired. I took it off and gave it to her. We parted crying.

~

The next morning, I had my last lesson with Pio and he took a last look at each of my dances. He rocketed me through all five, a whole repertoire in one hour, Julio demonized, Pio demanding all I could deliver.

It was not the personal Pio I studied with that morning. It was the maestro; and I couldn't complain.

He said no goodbyes to me. Nor I to him. I left the studio as if I would be returning the next day, and the next.

EPÍLOGO

Once my goodbyes were said, I didn't say them again, didn't
string out the parting in phone calls, notes, changes in plans.
However, as I left Sevilla, I did drive slowly past Pio's studio, past
the double-doors, past the dirty beige and green wall. The studio was
quiet.

~

I had decided to rent a car—one with a large trunk. Driving
to Madrid would cost me less than shipping my belongings back
home, I reasoned. Bypassing the Sierra Morena mountain range and
taking the more direct route to the capital through Extremadura, the
province along the Portuguese border, I would have time and money
enough to spend a couple of days in Madrid. But I hadn't counted on
the *paradores*, the castles and ex-convents of Spain converted into
government-run hotels.

The first town I came to was Merida; it had its *parador*. I
checked it out. The *parador* had been a sixteenth century convent. If
one can imagine a cozy convent, this was it. Downstairs was a busy
bar, an art gallery, a luxurious lounge, a great fireplace warming the
stone walls in the evening.

But with a convention in town of festival-minded, chattering
Spanish dentists, I was certain nothing would be available. Still, I
inquired if there was a room. There was—with a full breakfast, $28
a night.

Overlooking the lush central patio of the *parador*, my

generous room had upholstered armchairs, an antique writing desk, a walk-in closet with a full length mirror, an oversized twin bed, the sheets turned down at night with candies on the pillow.

And oh, the bathroom! Big, all-white tile, an enormous white bathtub. After a year of sitting in my tiny tub in my apartment with my chin on my knees, I would have paid twice, just for the bathtub.

I stayed two days in Merida, explored its Roman amphitheater still in use, its first century aqueducts, its mosaics, and with a religious holiday in progress, enjoyed the fireworks and folk dancing in the streets

Then I drove on to Trujillo through the landscape of Extremadura. Ghost-ridden, a perpetual mist over the ruins of castles, over low rock walls, every stone rounded to a curve by the winds, goats and sheep herded by men with straight backs and square jaws, their *gorras* pulled down over thick black eyebrows. A different Spain, I expected to hear bagpipes.

Trujillo was a bleak, quiet, uninviting medieval city. But here was another *parador*, also an ex-convent. Unlike Merida's, Trujillo's was austere. The lounge was silent, almost empty except for a nervous head housekeeper inspecting the edges of the rugs. Entering my room, I had to duck under its low doorway. The room, including the bathroom, was small, the furnishings spare. No cushions, no upholstery, no candies on the pillow.

Leaving Trujillo the next morning as a white sun bleached the sky, I turned eastward to Oropesa. Passing still another *parador*, I resisted the temptation to inquire, or even to eat in its restaurant. I stopped instead at an old *venta* for lunch. Its red tile roof had faded to orange; the overgrown grape arbor was slowly falling down. Inside, garlic braids and goat belly *botas* hung on white walls along with bright paintings of the Virgin. Behind the counter, an open leg of serrano ham, a few flies hovering, a little *mujer* cooking over a blackened stove. I relaxed; I was back in Andalucía.

I wanted a sandwich. The Spanish have no gift for sandwiches. To them it is a day-old dinner roll cut in half and spread with something thin, runny, and orange. I dictated to the man behind the counter:

"Bread first, *señor.*"

"*Sí, señora.* And with a little olive oil."

"No. No olive oil."

He paused, "If you say so, *señora.*"

"Now lettuce, *señor*, and a tomato. *Sí.* Now ham and cheese."

"With a drizzle of olive oil, *señora*?"

"No. But put another piece of bread on top."

"But, *señora*, it's already a meal!"

"Please. Bread on top."

"*Sí, señora,* if you say so."

As he put the bread on top, he picked up the bottle of olive oil. I said no. "Now, *señor,* cut the sandwich in half."

"Cut it? That will ruin it!"

"Cut it."

"*Sí, señora.* And a little olive oil?"

"No, *gracias.* Now what do I owe you?"

"Oh, *señora,* please, nothing. It's been an education."

~

Entering Madrid later that day, with less than twenty-four hours to connect with my flight, I turned my car in at the rental agency, unreachable except by driving the wrong way up a one-way street. I took a taxi to Mama and Papa Salinas' *pensión.* Full, they sent me around the corner to another. Checking in with the sweet-faced concierge, *Señora* Beatriz, I hauled my baggage out of the taxi, up the stairs, and into my room.

That's when it hit me. The room was hot and stuffy but sitting down on the edge of the bed, I started shivering. I had left Aurora, Heike, Joaquin, Lise, Mariano.

And Pio. How could I dance without him? All the ground we had covered, how could I have walked away from it? And when Pio had asked me to stay, I had cooly replied I wouldn't, as if I knew what that meant. What did I think I was doing?

Sitting alone in that silent room, the only answer I had was Rosario.

I recalled the day I saw him off at the airport. He had said, "When you get back, Doloré, we will do something together." Ready to throttle him, I hadn't replied then. Nor had I written him, nor expected anything from him. But I had kept an ear to the ground. Was he performing? He was. Did he have a company? He did.

It was dance with him, or, what? Go back to theatrical flamenco? Not likely. In California, Rosario would be my only connection to Sevilla.

The next morning, very early, I left Spain. Beatriz helped me put my bags in the taxi. Driving to the airport, I remember a cobalt blue sky over Madrid, black buildings and empty streets.

~

Home again, my upset feelings over Rosario did not change. But he carried the banner for *lo gitano*. He welcomed me into his flamenco company as if there were no strained relations between us. Perhaps in his mind, there were none. Glad to have a berth, I pretended there were none in mine.

I danced with Rosario for two years. As a company director and guitarist, he was as erratic as I had expected. He wouldn't show up for the rehearsals he had called; he changed the order of the programs as we walked onto the platform; he would set the tempos ridiculously fast or slow, because he felt like it. In the end, no one wanted him, not even the members of his own company. Asked to perform less and less, when he was finally not performing at all, no one noticed.

But for myself, I continued to dance. "Doloré," Pio once said to me, "I want you to carry on my choreography in California so everybody in the whole world will see what Pio Mateo Mendoza can do!" Glad to oblige, organizing my own flamenco company, I found venues on decks, in patios, in coffee houses and restaurants. I had a complete repertoire: *Alegrías, Siguiriyas, Soleá, Caracoles, Bulerías.* But closest to my heart was the *Siguiriyas.* Before I left Sevilla, Lise had said to me, "That is your signature dance, Doloré." She was right.

~

Pio, would often say of the Golden Age of flamenco, *"Ya no existe. Ya no existe."* But many things are *gone* since I left Spain.

Dear Aurora, who weighed 300 pounds when I last saw her, died thin. On a doctor's advice, she took up smoking to lose weight. It worked. She lost 150 pounds in two years—and died of kidney failure.

Despondent over her death, Pio threatened suicide many times. Once, he already had a leg out the window of a four-story building when a cousin of his walked in the room and said, with droll Gypsy logic, "If you're going to kill yourself Pio, you'll have to do it from a taller building."

Pio died of cirrhosis of the liver, or lung cancer—Rosario didn't know which—three years to the day after Aurora.

With Pio gone, the line of the old masters of flamenco closed down. But it continues in his students. Pio had the discipline, the knowledge, and the love for imparting his art. His new studio attracted many, and he taught well until the very end.

Old Teo, outliving both Pio and Aurora, finally did die. A quote from his nephew, Dieguito, at the funeral: "People are dying that haven't died before."

Heike, to whom I owe so much, refused chemo to extend her life.

Mariano. The gossip from Sevilla says his mind is gone. He knew the life of music, all of it, the painful details. But I remember him with lean hands balanced on the guitar in the light nights of Heike's patio.

There is good news: after twenty years of living together in sin, a delicious, wobbly, joyous sin, Joaquin and Lise were married.

~

I danced until I was 73. During that time, I began this book to hold onto what I might lose: I didn't want my memories to become the two-dimensional figures spilling out of a suitcase.

Now, far more important than performing is what I learned from Pio. Without thought, my body knows how to dance. It knows the exact angle my head should tilt, how to put the power of my thighs into my heels, how to coordinate the *compás* with the lilt of the singer's voice. My body knows the slant of the shoulders for a woman of turn-of-the-century Madrid, and how a Gypsy woman thrusts her breasts forward in the Bulerías.

None of this means I could do what I did in Pio's studio when I was fifty-five; it means it doesn't matter. Whatever move I make, it is right, it is whole. I have learned that when I dance, I am ageless.

As a dancer, I raise my arms in the kitchen and perform the

Siguiriyas for my frying pan. But as a writer, I cannot lift the words off the page to tell you the intense joy I feel when I dance.

abaniquería	The workshop of a fan maker.
abril	April
academia	School or studio
afición	Fondness
aficionado/a	A devoted follower of flamenco
aficionao	In the Andalucían dialect, a devoted follower of flamenco
Aiii...	The high-pitched opening wail in *cante jondo*
alegrías	A joyous dance, usually, but not always, a woman's dance
la americana	An American girl or woman
Anda!	Go for it!
andalus	The dialect of castilian Spanish which is spoken in Andalucía.
bailador/a	Dancer
baile	Flamenco dance
barrio	Neighborhood or district
bombones	Bon-bons, the nickname for butane cannisters
botas	Leather wine bottles, tradionally made of goat bellies
bulerías	A favorite *cante* of the Gypsies; it can be slow, fast, ribald, or raucous.
caballero	A gentleman
Calé	The Gypsies of southern Spain
Cálmate!	Calm down!
Caló	A dialect of the Andalucían Gypsies
canasteros	The traveling Gypsies of Spain
cante	A song, or the singing; the life-blood of flamenco
cante chico	The flamenco repertoire of light songs i.e., Alegrías, Bulerías, Caracoles
cante jondo	The repertoire of serious songs, i.e., Soleá, Siguiriyas, Saeta
cantor/a	Singer
cantao	Singer, in Andalu
caracoleros	Street vendors of Sevilla who sell snails

caracoles	Snails, a *cante* originating in Madrid or Andalucía, depending on who is talking.
casa chica	A married man's second family
caseros	Those Andalucían Gypsies who no longer travel.
caseta	The temporary houses of the April Fair
churros	Fried doughnut sticks
castellano	Castilian Spanish
Cómo?	What?
compás	The strict rhythmic underpinning of flamenco
el cojo	A crippled man
cordobés	A flat-crowned, formal riding hat
corrida	The bullfight
cuadro	The standard flamenco group consisting of singers, guitarists, *palmeros*, and dancers.
declamador	One who recites poetry in flamenco performances
dedicación	Dedication
Don Dinero	Literally, Sir Money, but said respectfully
doña	An older gentlewoman
duende	The spirit of flamenco that everyone talks about but no one can explain
duro	A coin worth about ten cents in 1985
Empezemos!	Let's get going!
en punto	On the dot, punctual
ensalada rusa	Potato salad
'Era casi na'	'It was almost nothing.' The highest compliment to a *cantor/a*
extranjero/a	A foreigner
el fenomeno	A star; a phenomenon
faena	The final act of the bullfight
farruca	An early flamenco song; the dance usually done by men to show off their heelwork.
feria	A fair
festival	Festival
fino	Dry sherry
los flamencos	Everyone involved in flamenco: aficionados, bailadores, cantores, declamadores, guitarristas, palmeros.

196

franquista	One who wishes for the return of fascism in Spain or, barring that, the return of Franco from the dead.
frío	Cold, as in November
gente	People
gitano/a	Gypsy
puro/a	Pure, as in pure-blooded Gypsy, or authentic, non-commercial flamenco
lo gitano	In the syle of the Gypsies
gorra	The ubiquitous visor cap, seen mostly in the countryside
gracia	Grace, gracefulness, graciousness
guajiras	A flamenco dance from Cuba
guitarrista	Guitarist
gusto	Enthusiasm.
Hace mucho tiempo.	It happened a long time ago; or it's been going on for a long time, depending on the context.
hidalgo	A gentleman of honor and good manners, often, but not always, an aristocrat
Hijo de Puta!	Son of a Whore! Not an *Hidalgo*
increíble	Incredible
jaleo	The verbal cheering of flamenco performers i.e., *Ole, Huzzah, Muchacha de España.*
la japonesa	A Japanese woman or girl
jipi	Hippie
juerga	An informal flamenco party
letra	Words or lyrics to a *cante* (song)
libertino	Lech
la lotería	The national lottery
machismo	Cult of masculinity
malagueña	A woman or girl of Malaga
manzanilla	Chamomile wine or tea
mare/pare	Mother or Father in Andalu
Mare de Dios	Mother of God! (*Madre de Dios* in Castilian)
marido	Husband
matador	Bullfighter
Me entiende?	Do you understand me?
me llamo	My name is
mi alma	My soul; a term of affection

mili	The military, refering to compulsory military service
monstruo	A phenomenon
motoncillo	A small shawl with a long fringe called a *fleco*
mujer	Woman or wife, depending on the context
muy buenos	Good day or good morning
la navidad	Christmas
Eh normal?	Is it normal?
no tiene remedio	It's hopeless; it can't be fixed.
noviembre	November
palmas	The rhythmic clapping of flamenco
palmeros/as	Those doing the *palmas.*
parador	Government run hotel or hostel
pasada	A step in the Sevillanas where two people pass each other back-to-back or front-to-front.
pasos	The floats of Semana Santa
payos	Non-gypsies, literally, 'clowns'
pesetas	The paper money of Spain before the Euro
penitentes	The penitents of Semana Santa
Pobre el Pio	Poor old Pio.
Por Dios!	For the love of God!
presumío	One who is presumptious, in other words, Pio
primo hermano	First cousin
pulpitos	Baby octopus
pundonor	Point of honor
puros	The authentic ones
puta	Prostitute
Más putas que ventanas	A saying: 'Sevilla has more prostitutes than windows.'
Que pena.	What a shame. What pain.
Qué te pasa?	What's bothering you?
rápida	Faster
más rápida	Even faster
rejoneo	Fighting bulls with a pole
rocío	Dew, refering to the pilgrimage to the shrine of *La Virgin del Rocío*
sabor	Flavor, essence, or quality
saeta	A votive song sung during Semana Santa

salón de fiesta	A nightclub for flamenco
semana santa	Holy Week preceeding Easter Sunday
Sevilla	Seville
sevillanas	The folkloric dance of Seville adopted into the flamenco repertoire
sí/si	'Yes', if accented. If not accented: him, her, maybe, or perhaps, depending on the context
Sígame.	Follow me. Do what I do.
siguiriyas	A formal ritualistic dance, or *cante,* with echos of the bullfight
silencio	The quiet, lyrical section of the *Alegrías*
sí mismo	Himself *(sí misma*—herself)
sinvergüenza	Someone shameless
sitio	A dancer's place on the stage
soleá	From *Soledad* meaning 'loneliness'
sombrillas	Window blinds
taconeo	The flamenco heelwork
tapas	Appetizers
tertulia	An informal gathering for discussion
toldo	Canvas awning
tortilla	An omelet, Spanish-style
traje de jinete	The formal riding attire of Andalucía
los ultimos	The greatest, the best
Vam'a bailar!	Let's dance!
Vaya con dios	Go with God, not shortened to *Adios* in Spain.
vecindad	Communal living quarters of the Gypsies
venta	Small country restaurant
verde	Green
vino verano	A wine cooler popular in summer
La vida!	Life!
Viva españa!	Long live Spain!
Que viva!	Yes!
Ya no existe.	It's all gone.
zarzuela	Originally stew; now, the light opera of Madrid

Author's Note

The expression, *"Aiii...,"* half-spoken, half-sung, has no literal translation. It conveys the emotional quality and anguish of the deep songs—the laments—of the *cante jondo* repertoire and the intense religious conviction of the *saetas*. Its origin is believed to be the early morning call to prayer of the Moslem religion.

Acknowledgments

There are many people I wish to thank for their encouragement and support, beginning with the late Rosalie Moore—teacher, friend, and mentor who, in no uncertain terms, told me to write this book and kept after me. I would like to thank my other writer friends in California, among them Barbara Brauer and Jean Pumphrey, who continue to offer me insight and direction. Evelyn Belvin and Kathleen Burgy have passed on, but they, along with Rosalie, Barbara, Jean, and I, met regularly to share our writing. Together we published two books of our poetry. When I moved to Oregon, Mary Brubaker introduced me to my current writing group, who are now both friends and critics: Fanda Bender, Gloria Boyd, Melissa Brown, Patricia Florin, Ellen Gardner, Addie Greene, Deborah Rothschild, and Dorothy Vogel. Sonja Ferrera and Marilyn Joy of the group have left Oregon and are missed. It was Ed Brubaker who introduced me to Roberta Kent, who has advised and encouraged me.

I would also like to thank Nancy Bardos for her photographic work on the book's front cover. And, especially, thanks to Nancy Parker, my computer guru, for her editorial support and direction in publishing.

About the Author

Dolores de Leon performed as a ballet dancer, modern dancer, and flamenco dancer in Los Angeles, San Francisco, New York, and Spain. She led and choreographed her own modern dance and flamenco companies in San Francisco. One of her ballets remains among the permanent repertoire of the Oakland Ballet Company. She taught modern dance at Dominican University in San Rafael, California.

As a writer, her short stories reflecting the lifesyle, belief systems, and traditions of the Gypsies of southern Spain have been published in the following literary journals: *Amoskeag, Arnazella, Convululus, Left Curve, The Madison Review, RiversEdge, Thereby Hangs a Tale,* and *Zahir.*

She served as an executive member of the Marin Poetry Center in San Rafael and a member of the Board of Directors of Intersection Art Center in San Francisco.

She now resides in southern Oregon.

The author dancing in a cramped studio in Sevilla.